RAZOR'S EDGE

SAVAGE HELL MC BOOK 6

K.L. RAMSEY

SAVAGE HELL MC

Razor's Edge (Savage Hell MC Book 6)

Copyright © 2022 by K.L. Ramsey

Cover Design: Michelle Sewell at RLS Images Graphics & Design

Formatting: Mr. K.L.

Imprint:Independently published

First Print Edition: April 2022

All rights reserved.

No part of this book may be reproduced, scanned, or distributed in any printed or electronic form without permission. Please do not participate in or encourage piracy of copyrighted materials in violation of the author's rights. Thank you for respecting the hard work of this author.

This is a work of fiction. Names, characters, places, and incidents either are the product of the author's imagination or are used fictitiously, and any resemblance to locales, events, business establishments, or actual persons— living or dead—is entirely coincidental.

RAZOR

Razor walked into the courtroom to meet his newest client. Savage had called to wake him in the middle of the night, to go downtown to help him out with a problem. He was supposed to meet with some woman who went by the name Firefly. He knew that her name was Penny Quinn, he just had no idea that Savage's little problem downtown would be Razor's walking wet dream, or that she was resourceful enough to get herself out on bail. He just hoped that she was going to be showing up at the arraignment, or his whole case was fucked. Hell, it was already fucked since he didn't even get the chance to talk to her yet about the case. She could be a total nut job, and he'd be fucked having to represent her anyway. He'd do it too because he owed Savage his fucking life.

He walked to the front of the courtroom and found a

pretty redhead sitting up before the judge's bench. He'd seen her around Savage Hell but never talked to her before.

"Firefly," he said, sitting down next to her. "Savage sent me."

"Of course, he did," she mumbled. "I've already told him that I'm good. I can handle things on my own."

He looked her over and nodded, "Of course, you can, but I'm a lawyer and I'd be happy to help you with your case. You know since I'm already here."

"That's so sweet of you," the redhead said. "But I think I'm good." She smiled at him, quietly watching as if her dismissing him would have him moving his ass out of the chair next to her. What the hell was he supposed to do now? He promised Savage that he'd help her, but if she refused his help, there was nothing that he could do. He'd just have to tell Savage that he tried and hope that the big guy believed him.

"Suit yourself," he grumbled. He got up from the table and walked to the row of chairs just behind where she sat, sitting down directly behind her.

"What do you think you're doing?" she whispered back over her shoulder.

"I'm not leaving until I have a report to give to Savage. He will want to know what happened to you and I plan on being able to tell him," Razor said.

"Fucking bikers and your stupid notions of duty," she mumbled. "I told you that I've got this," she insisted.

"And I told you that I'm not leaving here until I can tell

Savage what happened," he spat. The bailiff walked into the courtroom and told everyone to stand for the judge and Razor was just happy to get this shit show started. All he wanted to do was report back to Savage and go back to his bed. He hadn't had a good night's sleep for days and he was finally hoping to catch up on some much needed shut eye.

"Be seated," the judge said. "Is Miss Quinn present?" she asked.

"I am, your honor," Firefly said, standing from her seat.

"Where is your council, Miss Quinn?" the judge asked.

"I'm representing myself, your honor. I'm a third-year law student and feel capable of handling this," Firefly said. Well, that was news to Razor. He'd seen her around the bar, but never really asked too many questions about her. It was a good thing too because from the sound of it, she was much too young for him. He had just celebrated his forty-second birthday and well, she had to be about twenty-five. Razor was almost old enough to be her father.

"Well, you are in a bit of trouble, Miss Quinn," the judge chided. "You stole about thirty dollars' worth of groceries, and then when you were caught, you tried to punch the officer. Is that correct? How do you plead to the charges that I've just read to you?"

"Not guilty, with explanation, your honor," Firefly said.

"Let's hear it," the judge said.

"I've used my savings to pay for my last semester and had just enough left over to pay for my rent. I've recently lost my job and I was hungry. I only took enough to get by. I'm looking for another job right now, but no one is hiring since all of the college kids got back to town." Hearing that broke Razor's damn heart. He could tell that she was having the same effect on the judge. He'd been dead broke when he graduated from law school. He even held off on taking the bar until he could save up a bit of money. He didn't want to hope for a job as quickly as he was able to land one in the legal community.

"I see," the judge said.

"If I may, your honor," she said, holding up her hand as if she was in grade school.

"Yes," the judge said.

"I didn't attack an officer. I attacked a guard who worked security for the supermarket. I would never attack an officer of the law. The only reason I slapped the guard was because when he frisked me, he grabbed my ass. Legally, he's lucky I'm not suing him or the grocery store chain." She looked over to the table where the owner of the store stared straight ahead as if he hadn't even heard what she had just said.

"Is there any proof of this?" the judge asked.

Firefly smiled and nodded. "I recorded the whole thing on my phone, your honor," she said.

"Ah, technology," the judge breathed. "Let's see the footage," she ordered. The judge held out her hand for Firefly to approach and she did, removing her cell phone from her pocket and handing it up to her.

"It's the only saved video on my phone," she said. The judge found the one she spoke of and watched it, volume up at full, and the courtroom could hear the whole ugly scene as it played out. Razor could even guess when the guard had grabbed her ass in the video, hearing Firefly's gasp and then the sharp slap she administered, probably to the guy's face.

"Wow," the judge said, handing her back her cell phone. "Honestly, I would have slapped him too. Is this the kind of behavior that you approve of from your employees?" she asked the store owner.

"No," he said. "I had no idea that was happening when I told the head of my security to search her. But she stole from me," he insisted.

"I understand that," the judge said. "Please take your seat, Miss Quinn." Firefly walked back to the table and looked back at him just before taking her seat. Razor wondered what the look she shot him was about. Firefly sat down and faced the judge again.

"The way I see it, you have a choice to make," the judge spoke to the store manager and Razor had a good idea of how she might handle the situation. "You can press charges for the items that Miss Quinn took but didn't get away with. In which case, I'd advise her to press charges against your store and your employee for sexual harassment. Or you can drop the charges and hope that Miss Quinn is also in a forgiving mood and doesn't press charges against your store and your employee. What's it going to be?" she asked.

The store owner sighed and turned to his lawyer. The two men had a hushed conversation that seemed to go on for minutes, not just seconds, and then he stood with his lawyer.

"I'd like to drop the charges in exchange for Miss Quinn signing a statement that she won't press charges against my store," he said.

The judge looked back over at her, and Firefly seemed unsure. "Take it," Razor whispered from behind her. It wasn't the best deal, but it would do to get her out of trouble that could get her kicked out of law school or even keep her from taking the bar. This would keep Firefly's future safe.

"I'll take the deal, your honor," she agreed. "Thank you." The judge nodded, banging her gavel on the giant mahogany desk that she sat behind.

"Dismissed," she said. "Miss Quinn, I'd like to see you in my chambers," the judge said.

"Yes, your honor," Firefly breathed. She turned to look back at Razor, flashing him her sexy smile. "Guess I didn't need you after all," she sassed. She was a feisty one—he liked that attribute in a woman. No—she was a girl and much too young for him to be so attracted to her.

"It's not over yet, honey," he breathed, standing from his seat. "You still have to go back to chambers and that is usually not a good thing. You do know that she's not inviting you back for tea, right?" he asked.

The smile vanished from her face, and he almost felt bad for what he had just said to her—almost. "What do you think she wants?" Firefly asked.

He shrugged, "No clue. You want me to wait around?" he asked.

"No," she stubbornly whispered. "I've taken things this

far. I can go the distance." He pulled his business card from his jacket pocket and handed it to her. "The next time you need a little help, call me. I don't mind helping out an up-and-coming young lawyer. You shouldn't have to go without food just to be able to pay your tuition, but I've been there Firefly. You're not alone." Razor turned to leave the courtroom before he gave in to desire and asked her to go out to dinner with him. That wouldn't be a good idea for either of them and probably one she wouldn't entertain anyway. Right now, all he wanted to do was report back to Savage and have a few beers with his buddies. Then, he'd find a warm, willing woman to take back to his place to help him forget all about the sexy redhead with the sad eyes.

FIREFLY

Firefly was scared out of her mind as she walked back down the narrow hallway that led to the judge's chambers. The last thing she needed was a mark on her record before she even got done with law school. She knew better than to steal the food, but she was hungry and wasn't thinking straight. She was angry that her money had run out and that her father had told her that she was on her own. Hell, that shouldn't have come as such a surprise since she had been on her own for most of her life after her mother died.

She filed into the judge's chamber as the court bailiff held the door open for her. "Thank you," she said back over her shoulder to him.

"Yes, ma'am," he said. The bailiff shut the door behind her, and she looked around the office. It was very understated, quite like the judge, and sparse in furnishings.

"Miss Quinn," the judge said, entering the room from the side door. She had changed out of her dark robes and Firefly was surprised at how much smaller she looked in her street clothes. The woman was even wearing her sneakers with her business suit and Firefly wanted to giggle at her attire but refrained when the judge pointed to a chair.

"Have a seat," she directed. Firefly did as asked. "I'm sure that you're wondering why I've asked you to come back to my chambers."

"Just a bit," Firefly lied. She was shocked by the invitation and very curious. But her mother used to tell her that curiosity killed the cat, and well, she loved cats.

"I'd like to offer you an internship," the judge said.

"But—" Firefly started.

The judge held up her hand as if stopping her from speaking. "Please, just hear me out." Firefly nodded and she continued. "I admire the way that you held your own in my courtroom. I'd like to offer you a paid internship with my office. It won't be easy—especially with your coursework for the last year of classes, but I think that you'll be fine. Not all of us are lucky enough to receive scholarships, grants, or even have parents who are willing to pay our tuition. I was a lot like you while I worked my way through law school, and I know what it's like to be at the end of your rope. I want to ensure that you graduate, and I have a feeling that you might need a little extra help to do so. Will you take my job offer?" the judge asked.

Firefly didn't even have to think about it. This was an

opportunity that she couldn't pass up. "Yes," she almost shouted. The judge laughed and stood.

"Good," she said. "I'd like for you to start tomorrow," she insisted. "You haven't asked what the job entails or pays."

"Doesn't matter," Firefly insisted.

"I think you'll be pleased to know that not only is it a paid position, but you will also receive a partial scholarship from this office that will pay for the rest of your schooling, books, room, and board."

"That's too much," Firefly insisted.

"Not at all," the judge said. "As I've said, I've been in your shoes."

"Thank you, your honor," Firefly whispered, standing to shake the judge's hand. "For everything."

"See you tomorrow morning," the judge said.

"Yes," Firefly said. "You will." She left the office and walked back down the hallway to the courtrooms. As soon as she turned the corner, she ran right into the big lawyer/biker that she had seen around Savage Hell. It was her guilty pleasure, hanging out at that bar. God, she loved bikers, but she hadn't found one that she wanted to hang out with regularly.

She hung out with a few of the bikers—that was how she got her nickname Firefly. She loved her name and used it daily. When people asked her name, she'd tell them that it was Firefly, not Penny. She hated her birth name, and Firefly seemed to fit her better. The guys down at Savage Hell seemed to think so too, telling her that her fiery red hair helped them to come up with her name.

"I thought I told you that I was good," she said to the big guy. If she remembered correctly, his name was Razor. He was a little older than the guys she hung out with normally, but she had noticed him around the club.

"I told you that I wanted to be able to report back to Savage. He was the one who sent me down here to help you. Does he know that you don't need help?" Razor asked.

"No clue," Firefly said. She had met Savage years ago when she was just a kid. He was friends with her mother before she died and after she was gone, Savage took Firefly under his wing. Her father hated that she spent time at the bar, after she turned twenty-one, and maybe that was partially why she did it.

"Listen, I appreciate you sticking around, but I'm going to be fine. I was just offered a paid internship with the judge's office, and I took it. I won't be trying to shoplift food anymore and I'm pretty sure that you won't be getting any phone calls from Savage about me again."

"That's fantastic," he breathed. "Well, not the part about never hearing from you again. But the part about your internship here is great. You must have made quite the impression on the judge if she offered you a position like that."

She shrugged, "I guess."

"I'll let you go," he said. "I'm sure you have better things to do than to stand around talking all night. I remember how challenging law school was, even if it was eons ago."

"I doubt it was that long ago," she said. "Thanks for your

help, Razor," she said. He smiled at her, and she wondered if that had to do with the fact that she remembered his name. "See you around Savage Hell."

Razor nodded and started for the door and the next words were out of her mouth before she could decide if she should even say them or not. "Want to grab a beer with me now—you know, at the club?" she asked. God, she sounded like a bumbling idiot.

He paused in the doorway, hesitantly looking back at her. "I'm not sure that is a good idea, Firefly," he said. Hearing him say her name the way that he did made her feel a little giddy. "I'm a hell of a lot older than you."

She smiled back at him. "I really never let age factor into who I like to hang out with, Razor," she said. "It's just a beer—nothing more."

"Just a beer?" Razor asked.

"Yep," she agreed. "How about it?"

She felt as though she was holding her breath waiting for him to answer her, and when he finally nodded, she blew out her breath. "Just a beer," he agreed.

Firefly followed him out of the courthouse and when he walked her to her car and helped her in, she wondered if all older men were so chivalrous.

"I'll meet you over at Savage Hell," he breathed, dipping his head into her car. "Drive carefully." He shut her door and Firefly felt herself swoon—literally swoon and she shook her head at herself in her rearview mirror.

"Sounds good," she said. "I just need to stop by my apartment and then, I'll meet you over there." He nodded and shut her car door. "Get yourself together," she mumbled to her reflection. "It's just a beer."

RAZOR

Razor walked into Savage Hell and found Savage with his husband, Bowie, behind the bar. The place was packed tonight, and he guessed that Savage was lending a hand. Razor almost hated to interrupt his club's Prez, but he promised to give him an update and hopefully, he'd be able to fill Savage in before Firefly showed up to have a beer with him.

"Hey man," Savage said as he walked up to the bar. "Beer?" he asked.

"Sure," Razor agreed. He waited for Savage to pour the beer and hand it to him. "Thanks, man."

"I take it you went to court for Firefly today by the way that you're dressed," Savage said, looking him over. He hated wearing his suit and tie into the bar because of all of the shit the guys gave him, but he didn't want to take the time to run home to change since Firefly had asked him to meet for a beer.

"Yeah—but she honestly didn't need my help," Razor admitted. "Did you know that she's a third-year law student? In a few months, she'll be done and ready to take her bar exam, and then, she'll be a lawyer. She handled herself quite well on her own."

"I know she's almost a lawyer, but you know what they say about lawyers who represent themselves, right?" he asked Razor.

"Yeah," he breathed. "They have a fool representing them. I think that they say the same about doctors treating themselves too." He would never tell someone that they should represent themselves, no matter how good a lawyer they were. But he had to admit, Firefly seemed capable of handling herself.

"So, everything worked out then?" Savage asked.

"Yep," Razor said. "Firefly was even offered a paid internship with the judge who had her case. Apparently, I wasn't the only one impressed with her."

"That's wonderful," Savage said. "Listen, I appreciate you going down there for me. I know she's not one of our brothers, but I was friends with her mother before she passed away. I promised to keep an eye on Penny and when she called and told me that she was in trouble, I couldn't stand by and do nothing," Savage admitted.

"I get it," Razor said. "She seems like a great girl." That's how he needed to think about her too—like a girl and not a hot woman who made him want things he shouldn't want from her.

Razor looked across the bar when the front door opened, and Firefly walked in. Hell, every guy in that place turned around to check her out when she walked in, and he couldn't blame a single one of them. Firefly seemed to command attention when she walked into a room, just as she had when she won over the judge and the courtroom earlier today.

"I didn't think she'd be in today," Savage said.

"She asked me to have a beer with her to celebrate," Razor admitted.

"I see," Savage said.

"No, you don't see," Razor said. "It's not like that. She's a nice—"

"Girl," Savage finished his sentence for him.

"Right," Razor agreed. "She is and she asked me to have a beer with her tonight."

"So you said." Savage smirked at him, and he wanted to knock that smartass smirk right off his face.

"Can I just get two beers?" Razor asked.

"Sure," Savage agreed. He poured him two beers and handed them over the bar to him.

"Just start me a tab," Razor said. "And anything Firefly wants can go on it." Savage smiled at him and nodded, and Razor turned to walk across the room, running right into Firefly, pouring both of their beers onto the front of her.

"Oh crap," he breathed. "I'm so sorry." She looked down at

her soaked shirt and back up at him wearing an expression that looked a cross between pissed and amused.

"I swear, I didn't see you behind me, Firefly," he said.

"Um, it's fine," she said.

Savage stepped from behind the bar and handed her a t-shirt. "I have some extra shirts I keep here for emergencies. It's going to fit you more like a dress, but it's clean," he said.

"Thanks, Savage," Firefly said.

"You can change in my office. There's a lock on the door, use it. If these morons even think about you getting naked back there, they'll lose their minds."

"Lock the door—got it," she agreed. Firefly turned back to Razor. "Can we try this again when I come back out?" she asked.

"Um, of course," he agreed. He watched as she walked back down the dark hallway to Savage's office before he let a string of curses fly from his mouth.

Savage chuckled and clapped Razor on the shoulder. "Don't beat yourself up too badly," Savage said. "At least she asked for a redo." He was right, she had asked Razor to try having a beer together after she changed. He just hated that their night had started with him being a total moron.

"Can I get two more?" Razor asked.

"Yeah, but how about you go settle in my corner booth and I'll bring the beers over to you. I think it's best that you don't walk around the bar with them. I only have so many extra clean t-shirts."

"Ha, ha," Razor grumbled. "Thanks, man." He walked over

to Savage's private booth and settled in just as Firefly came out of his office.

"He was right, this is more like a dress than a t-shirt," she said, smoothing her hands down her body. He let his eyes follow their progress and nearly swallowed his tongue by the time she finished. All he could focus on was the fact that he wished it was his t-shirt that she was wearing after a night of hot sex. But that was going against his mantra about her being a "Nice girl."

"It looks nice," he lied. It looked so much better than nice, but he wasn't about to tell her that.

Savage brought over their beers and put them on the table. "Thanks for the t-shirt, Savage," she said. "And thanks for looking out for me today and sending Razor. I appreciate it—you're a good friend."

"No problem, Penny," he said. Savage was the only guy in the place that called Firefly by her real name. He was probably the only guy in the bar she'd allow that from. "Although I heard from Razor here that you really didn't need me to jump in to help out."

"Well, it was nice having someone in my corner," she said. "Even if I can take care of myself." Razor knew how she felt. It was one of the reasons why he loved his club so much. He knew that his brothers would always have his back.

Savage looked over his shoulder, back to the bar where Bowie was trying to flag him down. "I better get back over to help out before my husband has a coronary. I'm glad everything worked out, Firefly," he said. She nodded and watched Savage go back to the bar.

Firefly cleared her throat and smiled over at Razor. "Thanks for agreeing to meet me for a beer," she said. "I kind of wanted to celebrate and well, I don't really have too many people to celebrate with."

"No family?" Razor asked.

"Not really," she breathed. "My mother died a few years back and well; it was always just the two of us. My dad was kind of in and out of the picture. We still talk and he's helped out a bit with my tuition, but I guess you could say that he's back out of my life again." She shrugged, "Happens every time he gets a new girlfriend. I moved here to go to law school, and I don't make friends easily." Razor had seen her around the clubhouse more than a few times and every time he did, Firefly was surrounded by at least half a dozen guys.

"What about all of the guys here that follow you around?" Razor asked. He sounded as though he was accusing her of something and that wasn't his intent.

"Yeah, I get a lot of attention in here, but I was never interested in any of them. Honestly, I wasn't looking to become one of their ol'ladies. Drinking with them was one thing, but I'd never agree to go home with any of them. I didn't want to lead them on, you know?" she asked.

She was a smart girl. Any of the guys who took her home for one night would find a way to make her theirs. They'd come up with any excuse to stick around in Firefly's life because none of them would want to let her go.

"Well, I'll have a beer with you any time you need a drinking buddy," Razor offered. "No strings attached."

"Oh," she breathed. "What if I wanted strings, Razor?" she asked. She couldn't possibly mean what she just said to him. Had she just admitted to wanting him?

"I don't think that's a good idea," Razor admitted. "I'm old enough to be your father, honey," he admitted.

She shrugged, "I told you at the courthouse that I don't really care about age and all those stupid made-up rules, Razor. I've always kind of done my own thing."

"I get that," Razor said, "and, while I find that admirable, I can't say that I follow the same no rules policy."

"So, this is just the two of us having a drink then?" she asked, scotching closer to him. She was playing a dangerous game and from the smirk on her beautiful face, she knew it too.

"Yes," he whispered. Firefly was sitting so close to him; he could feel her warm breath on his neck.

"Liar," she accused. "I can almost hear your heart beating, Razor. You're either nervous or excited—maybe both, but I can tell that you want me."

"Do I?" he asked. He wasn't sure if he should deny what he was feeling for her or outright demand that she come back home with him tonight.

"You do," she insisted. "And I want you too, Razor. We're both consenting adults, so what's your hang-up here?"

He wanted to tell her that her age was a major hang-up,

but his cock was completely disagreeing with him. "No hang-ups," he said.

"Then, you're ready to admit that you want me?" she asked.

"I do," he agreed. He wasn't going to lie to her, not when she was offering her exactly what he wanted—namely, her.

"What are we going to do about you wanting me, Razor?" she teased.

"You're going to come home with me," he simply said. He wasn't asking her to come home with him—more like telling her, and she didn't seem to balk at his suggestion.

"All right," she agreed. "But this is going to be for one night and one night only," she insisted. "I told you earlier that I won't be anyone's ol'lady and I meant it. You good with that stipulation, councilor?" she asked.

"I believe that I am," he agreed. He'd say just about anything to get her into his bed at this point, even agreeing to just one night with her. Wanting more than that would make him sound like a greedy bastard, and he was, but Firefly didn't need to know that yet.

FIREFLY

She'd never saw a man drink down his beer so fast in her life. Razor seemed more than eager to get her out of Savage Hell and back to his place. "Where are you going to take me?" she asked.

"I have a house about ten minutes from here," he said. "Would you like to come home with me, Firefly?"

"I'd love to," she said. "Give me just a minute." She chugged down her beer and smiled back at him, wiping her mouth with the back of her hand.

"Jesus," he growled, "you might be the perfect woman, Firefly."

"That's sweet of you to say, Razor," she said. "But remember, no matter how perfect you find me to be, this is only for one night."

"Right," he mumbled. She wasn't sure if he meant it or

not. Hell, she wasn't sure if this was a good idea or going to be a colossal fuck up, but she'd find out soon enough because there was no way that she wasn't going home with him now.

"Let's go," he ordered. He stood from the booth and looked down at her, holding out his hand to her. Firefly could see every promise that he was silently making to her in his deep, blue eyes and she couldn't stop the little shiver that ran through her. There was something about Razor that made her half crazy with lust. He made her want to do things that she had never wanted to do with another man—namely, make him promises past tonight, but that would be a huge mistake.

Firefly took his offered hand, letting him pull her up from the booth and into his body. He wrapped an arm around her shoulder as if sending a clear message to the rest of the guys staring them down. She was his, if only for a night, and he was letting his brothers know it.

Razor waved back over to Savage, and she didn't miss the concern on his face as he watched the two of them leave the bar. Firefly wanted to tell him not to worry about her; that she was going to be just fine, but she didn't. Instead, she just nodded to him and smiled, trying to give him some comfort, but she wasn't sure how convincing she was.

"He's really protective of you," Razor said, holding open the door for her.

"Yeah, he is," Firefly agreed. "He promised my mom that he'd watch after me when she was dying. He was a good friend to my mom and now, he's a good friend to me. I appreciate him more than he'll ever know."

"See," Razor said. "You have family, he's just not related to you by blood, honey."

She shrugged, "I guess I never thought of it that way, but you're right." She had been alone for so long, but she knew that if she ever needed anything, she could call Savage and he'd be there for her, no questions asked. Razor was right, that would qualify him as family, even if she never thought of him that way.

Razor led her over to his car and held open the door for her. "I have my car here," she said. "I can just follow you back to your place," she offered.

"You promised me the whole night, Firefly," he said. "I want to make sure I get my full time with you. Let me drive you back to my place and in the morning, I can bring you back here to your car."

"I have school in the morning," she insisted as if she hated his idea. "I can't miss my class, since I missed today's classes. I only have three more months until I graduate and can take the bar. I don't want to fuck things up, Razor."

"I'll make sure that you get back here early enough to get to your class," he promised. "I wouldn't do anything to screw up you graduating on time, honey," he assured.

She nodded and slipped into his car. She just hoped like hell that Razor was sincere about not wanting to screw up her chance to graduate on time. She couldn't afford to pay another tuition payment, even with her new internship for the judge. All she wanted to do was pass her classes, take the bar, and find a good practice to hire her. It was her dream, and hopefully, one that would come true soon.

She watched as Razor walked around his car and slipped into the driver's seat. He seemed so calm and collected, she wondered if he did this type of thing often. "Do you bring a lot of women back to your place, Razor?" she asked.

He smiled over at her and shook his head. She could tell that he was lying, but Firefly let that slide. "I plead the fifth," he said. "If it makes you feel any better, I usually don't invite women back to my house. I usually end up at a hotel room or something. It's a privacy thing, I guess, but you feel safe to me."

"Thanks for that," she said.

"Well, I figured that you're good friends with Savage and if he likes you, then you must not be that bad," Razor said.

"Gee, thanks again," she teased. "I guess you're not so bad either, Razor."

"Thanks," he breathed. Razor pulled into a housing development that she drove by every morning on her way to class. She knew that a good deal of influential lawyers lived back there, and she dreamed that one day, she would too.

"You live back here?" she asked.

"I do," he said.

"I've always loved this development. The houses are gorgeous." Firefly looked out her window at the houses as they passed by. She never had the nerve to drive back into the part of the development that he was taking her into. "You live in the back?" she asked.

"Yep," he said. "It's more secluded back here. I feel like I have some privacy and the houses aren't as close together as they are up in the front of the development." Razor pulled into the driveway of a beautiful two-story brick home, and she couldn't help her gasp.

"This is gorgeous," she breathed. "I see why you don't usually bring women back here. They'd never want to leave," she teased. Poor Razor turned pale white when she said that, and Firefly couldn't help her giggle. "Don't worry, Razor," she said. "I'll leave in the morning. This is just for one night. Your gorgeous house won't change my mind about that."

"Right," he agreed. "One night and one night only." She wasn't sure if he sounded disappointed or if he was just repeating her words to her. Firefly knew better than to ask a man like Razor for more than one night. He just wasn't the settle-down kind of guy, and she wasn't ready to be settled either. No, this little arrangement was perfect. They'd both be able to blow off some steam and then, they'd just wave to each other when they saw the other at Savage Heat. They'd keep it casual and no strings—just what they both needed.

He got out of the car, suddenly quiet and reserved—so unlike Razor, and helped her out from the passenger side. "Thank you," she breathed, looking up at him. He was so big and tall, that she wondered if they'd actually fit together.

"I like it when you look at me like that, Firefly," Razor whispered.

"Like what?" she squeaked.

"Like you want to eat me alive," he breathed into her ear. God, the man smelled like heaven, and he was right, she did want to eat him alive. She just hoped that he would give her the chance to do just that.

He grabbed her hand and practically tugged her in through his garage door. "Are we in a hurry?" she questioned.

"I don't know about you, but I sure am," he growled. He grabbed her purse from her and tossed it onto his kitchen counter. "You want a drink?" he asked.

She should have told him yes since a drink probably would have steadied her nerves, but she found herself shaking her head as if she was just as eager as he was. "No," she whispered.

He crowded her space, pushing her up against the kitchen counter, and kissed her as if he was starving. "You taste so fucking good, honey," he whispered against her lips.

"You do too," she breathed. "I want to taste you all over, Razor," she brazenly admitted.

He groaned as she sunk to her knees in front of him, and she felt a heady power that honestly, she could get used to. She looked up at him while she unzipped his pants, silently pleading with him not to stop her. When she pulled his pants down his thick thighs, she found that he wasn't wearing boxers and his cock bobbed out at her, almost begging for her to touch it.

"You're big," she said. It sounded like a praise, and maybe

it was, but she still worried that they wouldn't fit together. She ran her hands over his shaft, and he moaned and thrust himself at her as if asking her for more. She didn't need him to give her the orders, she knew what he wanted next from her. Firefly licked the head of his shaft and another moan ripped through his chest. She loved the effect that she seemed to have on him. It made her feel powerful and wanted. She let the head of his cock slip past her lips and when she sucked him to the back of her throat and swallowed around him, he seemed as if he couldn't take her being in control anymore. Razor grabbed handfuls of her hair and worked his cock in and out of her mouth, taking over the blow job. She loved the way he took control, taking what he needed from her. He didn't give any warning as he came down her throat. She knew that he'd expect her to take every last drop of him and she did, not wanting to disappoint Razor.

He pulled free from her mouth, panting as though he had just run a marathon. "Baby," he crooned. Razor helped her up from the floor and lifted her into his arms, sitting her up on the kitchen counter. "Your turn," he whispered. He kissed his way down her body, removing her clothing as he went and before she knew it, she was sitting completely naked on his countertop, waiting for whatever he planned next for her.

"You're so fucking sexy," he growled. He pulled her to the edge of the countertop and spread her legs over his shoulders. Razor didn't waste a minute, he dipped his head and ate her pussy, making a meal out of her. It had been so long since she had been with a man, she forgot how good it felt to have someone eat her the way Razor was. Her vibrator would never feel adequate again. Firefly lost count of how many orgasms he had given her, and when he finally finished with her, she felt as though she was flying.

"Firefly," he said, standing to his full height in front of her. She felt as though she couldn't focus. "Look at me, honey," he ordered. She looked up his body to his gorgeous blue eyes and smiled. "You on the pill, baby?" he asked. She nodded and hummed, not quite ready to speak.

That was all the answer Razor seemed to need as he pulled her into his arms. When her back hit the cold wall, she hissed out her breath and Razor slammed into her body, his cock filling her.

"Oh God," she moaned, "you feel so good."

"You do too, baby," Razor rasped. He pressed her into the wall, and she felt as though it might swallow her up. He wasn't gentle, and that was just fine with Firefly. She always liked sex a little rough and Razor delivered. He pumped into her body as she rode out another orgasm and after she shouted out his name, he followed her over finding his own release. Razor kept her pressed against the wall, kissing her and whispering little praises, and she thought for sure that she'd never find another man as perfect for her as he seemed to be. But that was a dangerous thought and one that she shouldn't entertain. She had been very clear that they were going to be together for one night and one night only. Thinking about him long-term couldn't happen. She wouldn't break her own rules, not even for the perfect man, no matter how much she hated herself for it.

Three Months Later

Firefly walked into the judge's chambers, not really sure what she was going to say or do. Finding out that she was pregnant wasn't what she had hoped for, but now that she knew for sure, she was happy and scared out of her mind, all at the same time. How the hell was she going to take care of a baby? The better question was how she was going to tell Razor that their one night together had ended up with one very unexpected surprise.

She had woken up sick every day for the past month and a half. If she hadn't been knee-deep in finishing her classes, wrapping up papers, and taking her finals, she might have noticed earlier, but she hadn't. She just thought that she was burning the candle at both ends—something Firefly was used to. She was going to school full time, practically working a full-time job, and avoiding the man she never stopped wanting, even if they had agreed to only one night. Yeah, she was busy, so she thought that was the reason why she had been puking her guts out every morning. It wasn't until her finals were finished and she had walked across the stage to receive her degree, that she realized that a baby was a possibility, even though she was on the pill. And one pregnancy test later, she knew for sure.

Telling Razor was something that she thought about doing, but the night that they hooked up, she was adamant about it only being a one-night thing. Telling him that he was going to be a daddy would lead to a whole lot more than he signed up for. Plus, to tell him about the baby, she'd actually have to see him, and she hadn't seen or heard from him in the three months since they had slept together.

At first, Firefly was the one who avoided going to Savage Hell. Savage had even called her a few times to check on her and see if she was all right. Firefly came up with a few excuses, most of them involving her new internship or her course workload for law school. After a while, Savage seemed to give up and stop calling her every week. Then, one night, she was feeling lonely and missed hanging out at the bar, so Firefly went into Savage Hell after work and that's when Savage told her that Razor hadn't been in for a while either. He admitted that he believed the two of them had gotten together and taken off or something, and she laughed it off. But a part of her wished that it was true. Their one night together had changed her in more ways than one. She never wanted a relationship with any man, but Razor had her thinking about the possibilities. Hell, she never thought that she wanted kids before, but getting pregnant with his baby had her rethinking her whole life.

She'd gone in a few times a week after that and each time, she hoped that she would run into Razor. What she'd do if that happened was still a mystery to her, but she was still hopeful. But he never showed. The guys would offer to buy her a beer, but she knew that they were only after one thing and the only man she wanted wasn't there. So, she'd hang out with Savage and casually ask if he'd heard from Razor, but he never did. No one had and now, she was going to have to face being a single mom and somehow find time to pass the bar so that she'd be able to practice law. It was the only way she'd be able to take care of her new baby because she had no one else to lean on throughout her pregnancy.

Honestly, she knew what she had to do—leave town. If Razor didn't want anything to do with her, she could take a hint. But she wouldn't hang around town, hoping that at some point, he'd show up and take an interest in her again. If she wasn't good enough to be there for, then her kid wasn't either. She hated that her kid was going to have to grow up without a father. Her dad was mostly absent from her life, and she turned out all right with just a mom, and so would her kid. She'd raise her baby alone, and never look back at this town or her life. But first, she'd have to break the news to Judge Josephs. Then, she'd finish packing up her crappy little apartment and head out of town. She had no idea where she'd land or what she'd do until she passed her bar, but that was fine with her. Firefly couldn't stand spending another night in a town that harbored a man who had stolen her heart, and then avoided her like she had the plague.

She walked into the judge's chambers and found her sitting behind her desk. "Judge Josephs," she said.

"Oh, hi Penny," she said. It was a fight to get the judge to stop calling her "Miss Quinn". Trying to get her to call her

Firefly was almost comical, and when they agreed to Penny, she was just happy that the judge was fine with dropping some of the formalities in their relationship.

"You're here early," Firefly said.

"I have a full docket," the judge said. "You're not supposed to be here today. In fact, you have a few weeks off to celebrate your graduation."

"Yes," Firefly said. "I got the card and gift that you sent me. You didn't have to do that." The judge had sent her a generous gift and now, she planned on using it to help pay her way in the world until she could figure her shit out.

"I'm glad that you received it. And, it was my pleasure," the judge said. "So, what has you coming in on your day off?" she asked, cutting right to the chase.

"I have to leave town," Firefly said.

"Oh?" the judge questioned. "For how long?"

"Permanently," she said, noting the disappointment in the judge's face. "I'm sorry, but something has come up. I can't stay here. I guess you could say that I need a fresh start."

"We've all been in that place, Penny. I've told you that you and I have had a very similar life. I struggled to make my way through law school. I guess that's why I took you under my wing the way that I have," she said.

Firefly nodded her head. They had talked extensively about how similar their lives had been, but there was one difference now that she wouldn't be able to overlook for very long. She was beginning to show a little bit and soon, others would notice too. She needed to be long gone before that happened.

"Did you ever have any kids, Judge Josephs?" she asked.

"No," the judge said. "I never married and never had any children, but that was a choice that I made. I know plenty of women lawyers who have families and a healthy work life. It's possible if that's what you're worried about, Penny," she said.

"It's kind of what I'm worried about," she admitted. "But with a twist. You see, I'm not married or even with anyone, but I am going to have a baby in about six months. I just can't stay in town. I can't take the chance of the father finding out about this baby," she said, cupping her barely-there tummy.

"I see," the judge said. "If you don't mind me asking, is there a reason why you can't tell the father?" she asked.

"He's not a good man," she lied. The judge wouldn't understand that she wasn't going to tell Razor because she made him agree to just one night together. The fact that he was avoiding her now didn't make him a bad guy either, really. He had no idea what he was avoiding, and if she left town without telling him, he never would know.

"Can I do anything to help? Maybe a restraining order or something like that," the judge said.

"I appreciate that," Firefly said, "I really do, but I need to do this. I need to leave town." She left out the part about being heartbroken over the fact that Razor was avoiding her or that she had possibly fallen for the guy in just one night of being with him. Yeah—those things would be what she kept to herself. No one would ever hear those truths from her—ever.

"While I can't say that I understand, I will respect your feelings and wishes," the judge said.

"Thank you, Judge Josephs. I appreciate that." She stood by the door, not sure what her next move should be. The judge stood and rounded her desk, pulling Firefly into her arms for a quick hug.

"I wish you only the best," the judge said. "Both of you."

Firefly felt a bit choked up and the last thing she wanted was to run out of the judge's chambers sobbing like a moron. "I need to clean out my desk," she said. "I'm sorry that I won't be able to give you two weeks' notice, but I can't stick around town and take the chance that someone will notice my growing belly."

"Don't worry about the two weeks. Will you at least let me know when you've gotten settled? I'd like to forward your last paycheck to you," the judge said.

"Sure, as long as you promise me never to share that address with anyone," Firefly insisted.

"I think I can make you that promise," the judge agreed. "It's been a pleasure working with you, Penny. Promise me that you'll still take your bar exam," she demanded.

"I plan on it," Firefly said. "In fact, I hope to take it before the baby gets here so that I can have a job lined up after my maternity leave is over."

"That sounds like a good plan. I'd be happy to give you a good reference, if you need one," the judge said.

"I will keep that in mind," Firefly agreed. "Thank you—for everything." She walked out of the judge's chambers, trying to keep her tears at bay. Right now, she planned on grabbing her things from her tiny cubby space, and then, she'd go home to cry her eyes out.

RAZOR

Two Years Later:

Razor walked into Savage Hell and could feel all eyes on him. "What the hell?" he asked. "Why's everyone staring me down?" Most of the guys had avoided him over the past couple of years. They caught on that he was a bit rougher around the edges—meaner even, but it had nothing to do with the guys in his club. Honestly, it had to do with one woman who had completely disappeared from his life. That's what had made him so grumpy and anyone who had a problem with that could kiss his ass.

Savage walked across the barroom and stood in front of Razor. "We need to talk," he said.

"Talk about what?" Razor asked.

"Firefly is back and well, she has someone with her," Savage said.

He knew that someday this could happen. She was a young, beautiful woman, and any man would be damn lucky to have her. It was only a matter of time before she came back home with a new man—or maybe even husband. Razor wanted to kick himself for agreeing to her stupid stipulation about their night being a one-time deal. If he could go back and do it all over again, he'd tell her to take her stipulations and shove them up her ass. He was so eager to get her into his bed, that he overlooked the fact that he might develop feelings for her. Hell, he hadn't planned on falling for her in just one night together, but that's exactly what happened. The only way that he could keep his promise to her was to completely avoid her, no matter how much doing that ripped her guts out.

"While I'm happy she found someone, I don't really want to see her with anyone else, man," Razor said. Savage was one of the only people in his life who knew what Firefly leaving did to him. He was messed up for a damn long time. Hell, he still had trouble picking up women and not comparing them to her. After a while, he just gave up and that was plain pathetic.

"I think you'll want to see her and meet the new guy in her life," Savage assured.

"I'll pass," Razor challenged.

"Don't be a pussy," Savage said. "She's here with her son, not some dude."

"Her son?" Razor asked.

Razor's Edge

"Yeah—her one-year-old son and he has your eyes, man," Savage whispered that last part.

"Shit," Razor grumbled. "Are you telling me that the kid is mine?"

"Don't know for sure," Savage admitted. "Why not ask Firefly?" There were many reasons why he shouldn't ask Firefly if she had his kid and kept it from him—the very first being that would mean he'd have to see her again, and that was something that he had been trying to avoid for almost two years now.

Razor started back to Savage's office, making his way through the crowd of bikers. "Go easy on her," Savage shouted. "She looks like she's been through hell and back."

Razor waved over his shoulder, "No promises," he shouted back. If she had been keeping his kid from him, he wouldn't care what she had been through.

He didn't bother to knock before walking into Savage's office. He walked in and found Firefly sitting on the big leather sofa that Savage kept in his office; a little boy sitting on her lap, smiling up at her. God, Savage was right, the kid looked just like him—blue eyes and everything.

"Is he mine?" Razor growled. She looked up at him and nodded. She did look like she had been through hell and for just a minute, he thought about going easy on her.

"What the fuck, Firefly?" he asked.

"Can you please not cuss in front of my son?" she asked.

"He's my son too. You just admitted that, honey. How could you keep him from me? I had a right to know that you were pregnant," Razor said. He would have done right by her and his kid, but she hadn't given him the opportunity to do that.

"You took off and I didn't see you again," Firefly said. "I came by the bar for weeks on end and you never showed up again. I even went by your house a few times and you weren't there—or maybe you just didn't want to answer. How was I supposed to tell you about him?" she said, nodding to their son. "You never gave me that chance."

"You were the one who said that you only wanted one night with me, Firefly," he said. "If I had shown back up to Savage Hell, I would have broken my promise to you, so I had a few of the guys helping me keep a look out for you. If you were there, I made sure that I wasn't. I thought that it was the easiest way to keep my promise to you and give you time at the bar."

"So, you were intentionally avoiding me then," she whispered.

"At first, yes. I was trying to avoid you because I knew that if I saw you again, I'd want you. Hell, I've wanted you for the past two years, but I couldn't find you. And believe me, I tried," Razor admitted. When he found out that she had packed up her apartment and left town, just months after they were together, he asked everyone who knew her where she had gone. Savage swore he didn't know, and he believed his friend. Firefly was a smart girl, and she knew that telling Savage where she was going would end up with Razor finding out. Plus, she wouldn't put Savage in the middle.

He exhausted every possibility, tracking down everyone who personally knew Firefly, including her former professors. No one knew where she was or why she had left town so abruptly. He finally got around to going to the judge who had given Firefly a job, and she told him that she hadn't heard from Firefly since she left town. He could tell that she knew more than she was letting on, but he didn't push. Instead, he left her chambers resolved to give up—and that plain sucked.

Razor tried to get back to his life, finding a rhythm that worked for him—a balance between work and his private life, but it never came. He threw himself into his work and practically lived and breathed his job, giving up on his private life being more than going back to his house to sleep. He was lonely and more than that, he was resolved to stay that way because if he couldn't have Firefly, he didn't want any woman.

"I know," she whispered. "The judge called to tell me that you had been asking about me."

"So, she knew where you were?" he asked.

"Yes, she was the only person that I told about leaving town and about Garret," she said.

"You gave him my name?" he asked. She was one of the only people that he ever told his real name to. Everyone else knew him as Razor, but during their one night together, he told her that his name was Garret Tracy. They shared a lot of things with each other that night. A part of him hoped that she'd give him a chance, maybe even ask him for another night or more, but she hadn't. Instead, she left the next morning, apparently taking more than just a piece of his heart with her.

"I did," she whispered. "I hope that's okay."

He nodded, feeling too choked up to answer her. "Can I hold him?" he asked.

"Sure," she agreed. "He's a little fussy because he's overly tired."

"I don't mind," he said. "I'd like to meet my son." Firefly stood and handed the baby to him. God, he was so tiny and so damn cute, he instantly lost his heart to the little guy. Garret looked up at him, giving him a blank stare as if fascinated by him. He reached up and tugged Razor's beard and he winced, causing the little guy to giggle.

"He likes you," Firefly said.

"Why didn't you tell me about him?" he asked. "You could have told Savage and he would have tracked me down."

"The night that we were together, I promised you that it was only going to be for one night. I never imagined that it would lead to me getting pregnant and I didn't want you to be a part of our lives because you felt obligated to be."

"You wouldn't have been an obligation, Firefly. Neither of you would have been an obligation," he said, looking down at his beautiful son.

She swiped at the tears that spilled down her face and he hated that he had made her cry. "I was on the pill," she breathed. "This shouldn't have happened, but my doctor said that sometimes, nature just finds a way. I had no idea that I was pregnant until my second trimester. I was so busy finishing law school and working for the judge, I overlooked the fact that I was throwing up every morning for the first three months of my pregnancy. I thought that I had caught a bug, and when it didn't go away, I thought that I was just overly stressed and working too hard. I had no clue that I could possibly be pregnant—that didn't occur to me until I graduated, and things settled down a bit. I realized that I hadn't had a period for a few months, which usually isn't a big deal for me since I was never really regular. I bought a pregnancy test and when it came back positive, I went to my doctor to confirm that it was true."

"You must have been scared out of your mind," Razor said. "I know I would have been. You didn't have to be alone though."

"I was scared," she admitted. "I was going to tell you," she whispered. "I came into Savage Hell that night, looking for you, and Savage said that he hadn't seen you for weeks. I guess that was the night that made it very clear to me that you were purposely avoiding me. I took the hint and stopped trying, but I had to come up with a plan. I knew that if I stuck around town, I stood the chance of running into you. If that happened when you were out with another woman, it would have devastated me. I knew that I needed a fresh start, so I left town." Knowing that she planned on telling him about the baby, but he was being an asshole and hiding away from her like a coward, made him feel like shit. If he would have just come clean with her that he wanted more than one night with her, things might have been different.

"I was a coward," he breathed. He looked down at little Garret who was asleep, cradled in his arms, and smiled. "Everything would have been so different if I had just found you and admitted that I wanted you for more than just one night. I was so afraid of telling you that; of breaking the rules that you put in place for our night together, I went and fucked things all up." She looked down at Garret and back up at him as if reminding him that cussing around their son wasn't an option. "Sorry," he whispered. "I guess it's going to take me some time to get used to little ears being around."

"You wanted more than one night with me?" she asked.

"I did," he said. "It's why I avoided you. God, I was an idiot."

"No," she said. "I was the fool. I put that stupid stipulation in place when I didn't want it there, to begin with. I was just trying to protect my heart. I didn't believe that you'd want me for more than a night, so I came up with that stupid rule to try to convince you to be with me. And now, it's probably too late. I mean, you have to have a girlfriend or a woman in your life, right?"

He chuckled, making Garret squirm in his arms. He almost felt as though he was holding his breath until the baby settled again. "I haven't been with a woman in two years, honey. Since you, I haven't found another woman I wanted to be with. Lord knows that I tried, but no one appealed to me. I threw myself into my work trying to forget you."

"Did you?" she asked. "Were you able to forget about me, Razor?" she asked.

"No," he growled. "I don't think that was even a possibility."

She nodded, "You might change your mind when I tell you why I'm here," she said.

"Why did you come back to town now, after all this time, Firefly?" Razor asked.

"I need your help," she said. "I'm in danger and I can't let it touch Garret. I need for you to take him while I work this all out."

"Take him?" Razor asked. "You want me to take our son and let you walk back into danger to handle it on your own?" he asked.

"Yes," she said.

"What kind of danger are we talking about here, honey?" Razor asked.

"When I left town, I was almost four months pregnant. I knew that I had only a few months to pass the bar so that after the baby was born, I could hit the ground running and find a good job. I moved to Boston, knowing that there would be a ton of choices for me to find a good job at a law firm. I did too. I started as a junior lawyer at one of the top firms in the Midwest. I was happy and I loved my job. I found a good daycare for Garret, and we have a cute little apartment. The only thing missing from my life was you,

Razor. So many times, I thought about picking up the phone and calling you to tell you about him, but I was scared."

"Scared of me?" he asked.

She shrugged, "Not so much you, but how you would react. I didn't want to lose him if you came at me for full custody of him. On the other hand, I worried that you'd want nothing to do with him and that someday, I'd have to tell our son that his father didn't want him." He wanted to tell her that not only did he want their son, but he also wanted her, but he wasn't sure if Firefly was ready to hear that truth from him.

"Honestly, I don't know how I would have reacted two years ago. I was bitter that you seemed to go on with your life while I wanted another shot with you," he said.

"That's not true," she said. "Hell, I spent most of my days trying to figure out how to get you to notice me. First, I had to find a way to be in the same room with you again, but that never happened. You were pretty good at avoiding me."

"Well, I did have a couple of the guys keeping an eye out for you," he admitted. "If you showed up here, I'd get a text telling me to steer clear, so I did. I guess I never imagined this happening," he said, looking down at his son. "I never thought that I'd be a father and that avoiding you would cost me a year of my son's life."

"I'm sorry," she whispered. "I should have tried harder to find you, Razor," she said. "I just didn't know what to do."

"And I should have acted like a grown-up and showed up. Instead, I hid away from you and my feelings for you. I guess we're both to blame, honey," he said. "But you still haven't told me what has you so fired up."

"Right, sorry," she breathed. "I got sidetracked. Where was I? Oh—I got the job as a junior lawyer and started to take on cases at my new firm in Boston. I was doing great and well, they moved me up pretty quickly. Before I knew it, I was handling one of my first big clients. I didn't know it at the time, but my client was involved with one of the biggest crime families in Boston. He was looking at doing time for grand theft and attempted murder and I was supposed to get him off. At first, I was really excited to be getting my first big profile case, but then, I started receiving threats that if I didn't keep my client out of jail, my life and my son's life were over. I went to my boss, and he insisted that I keep the threatening text messages to myself. He said that going against that family would end badly for me and Garret, so I kept my mouth shut."

"Shit," Razor cursed. "Tell me you eventually went to the cops," he demanded.

"No," she breathed. "Not until it was too late. I started getting those same messages sent to my home, via a carrier. They would be delivered to my apartment door and when I'd ask who the sender was, the delivery guy couldn't give me an answer. That's when I went to the cops. I was worried that my boss might be in on whatever was happening to me, and I didn't want to take any chances."

"Good," Razor said. "What did the cops do?"

"Nothing," she said. "They took the messages from me, confiscated my phone, and told me that they'd look into it."

"What the hell?" Razor growled.

"It gets worse," she said. "Two days ago, I got home from work after picking up Garret from daycare and found that my apartment had been broken into. The place was ransacked and there was a newly written message telling me that if I went to the cops again, my son would pay the price. That's when I packed up as much as I could fit into my car and drove back here to Huntsville."

"You drove from Boston back to Alabama with a baby—all by yourself?" he asked.

"Yep," she said. "It was a damn long trip and Garret fussed for at least half of it. I'm still nursing him, and we kept having to stop so that I could fee him. I think he's going through a growth spurt. I came right here and asked Savage to help me find you. I can't take Garret with me back to Boston, they'll kill him."

"You're not going back to Boston either, honey," Razor insisted.

"I have no choice," she said. "My case goes to court next week and if I'm not there to represent my client, I could be found in contempt. Worse than that, the family that he works for will come after both Garret and me, and I can't let that happen. No matter what happens to me, I need to know that my son will be safe."

"Our son will be safe, and you will be too. I won't let you go back to Boston alone. I won't make the same mistakes that I've made in the past. I let my stubborn pride get in the way once, I'm not about to let that happen again, honey," he said.

"What are you suggesting?" she asked.

"Let me do a little bit of digging and hopefully, we can come up with a way to get you excused from the case," Razor said.

"I don't know," she said. "If I let you get involved, that will put you in danger too."

"I don't give a fuck about me, honey," he said. "How much do you know about this guy that you're representing?" he asked.

"Everything," she breathed. "He's guilty as sin and I can prove it. I think that's why the threats started in the first place. I started looking into things that I wasn't supposed to. He was so careful and calculated about what he told me; I didn't believe a word he was saying. That's how I found out that he was working for the Manzoni family. I started to snoop around some more and found out that he not only did what he's being accused of but there's also video footage of him doing it. He's also heavily involved in the family's biggest venture—human trafficking. If he goes away, they lose a major delivery pipeline that's being run through him."

"What's the guy's name?" Razor asked.

"Marcos Francoli," she said.

"Where is this evidence you have on him?" Razor asked.

"I sewed the thumb drive, with the video footage on it, into the lining of my diaper bag," she admitted.

"Smart girl," he said. "You have to turn that footage over to the state's attorney's office, Firefly," he said. "It's the only way to make sure that this creep doesn't get off. If he walks, you'll never get your life back."

"Even if he doesn't walk, the Manzoni family has promised to come after me. I'm as good as dead in either scenario," she said around a sob.

"I'm not going to let that happen, honey," he promised. He meant it too. There was no way that he'd let anyone touch her or his son.

"I can't ask you to get involved," she said.

"Too late," he growled. "I'm already involved and there is no way that I'm going to let our son grow up without his mother. I had that life and it's not something that I want for him. Grab your stuff," he ordered. He put his sleeping son into his car seat and buckled him in.

"Where are you taking us?" she asked.

"Back to my house," he said. "Would anyone be able to link us together?" he asked.

"Um, I don't think so," she breathed.

"Am I listed on Garret's birth certificate?" he asked.

"Shit," she mumbled. "Yes, you are."

"Then, we'll have to move fast. We'll go back to my place so that I can pack up some things, then, we'll head out of town."

"Out of town?" she asked.

"Yeah, a buddy of mine has a plane and he'll fly us out of here. We just need a place where we can lay low for a bit until we figure this all out, but there's no way that you're walking back into that courtroom," he said. She nodded, looking completely defeated, and Razor pulled her into his arms. "I've missed you, Firefly," he breathed, gently kissing her lips. She tasted just the way he remembered and that only made him want her even more. They'd get to that soon enough. Right now, he just needed to get her and Garret someplace safe. Then, he'd convince her to give him more than just one night.

FIREFLY

Moving north wasn't her first choice, but when she left Alabama, she felt that going to Boston was her best chance at finding work. She hated the winters and longed to move back to Huntsville but was scared out of her mind about having to tell Razor that he was a father. She worried that he'd never be able to forgive her for not telling him about Garret. Instead, he was being so sweet to her, and seeing him holding their son did strange things to her heart. She knew that keeping her little boy from his father wasn't her best idea, but she really had no clue what to do about any of this. She felt as though she had been floundering since finding out that she was pregnant and hadn't made one good decision since the day she peed on the pregnancy test, sealing her fate.

When Razor told her that he hadn't been with any other

woman since her because he never wanted anyone but her—well, that gave her some crazy hope that she shouldn't be allowed to have. Hope was dangerous now that she was a single mother. It was something that gave Firefly a false sense of security, and she didn't need that on top of everything else she had going on with the court case and threatening letters that she had been receiving. She needed to keep her head in the game and think through her next step, not dream about a life that could have been if she hadn't put stipulations on their night together. Dreaming about what-ifs was a dangerous game and one that she refused to play now that she was a mother. Garret was depending on her to find her way through this mess and keep him safe. That's the reason why she went home—to ask Savage for his help. She just never expected to find Razor at Savage Hell or to dream that he'd be willing to help her.

Now, Razor had her rushing out of the bar and she felt as though all eyes were on her. He carried Garret in his car seat and damn if that didn't make her heart do a little flip flop in her chest.

"Wait here," Razor ordered, and she didn't dare protest. She needed his help and if she had to follow the commands that he barked at her, she'd do it. He walked over to Savage and the two talked while she waited by the front door. The two seemed to go back and forth behind the bar and then Razor shook Savage's hand and he rejoined her at the door.

"We're good to go," Razor said.

"What's happening?" she asked.

"Just what I said earlier," he breathed, ushering her out of the bar and into the warm night's air. It was still freezing up in Boston but down here, the air felt as though summer was about to burst onto the scene. It made her realize how much she missed the warm spring nights in Alabama.

"We're stopping by my place to grab some of my things, and then, we're meeting Ryder at his hanger. He's a pilot and has a plane. He's going to fly us to a little cabin that Savage has, up in West Virginia. His grandfather recently passed away and left it to him. He says that it's rustic but will work in a pinch to keep us on the down-low."

"That's sad that his grandfather died," she said. Firefly suddenly realized that she had missed so much by leaving town. Everyone's lives went on and she wasn't a part of them. It was probably how Razor felt when he found out that he had missed the first year of his son's life.

"He didn't know the guy. Hell, until Savage got the letter from his grandfather's lawyer, telling him that he had inherited the cabin in West Virginia, he didn't even know that the guy existed."

"That's sad," she whispered. He walked to her car, letting her trail behind him and she could tell that he had something that he wanted to say, but wasn't.

"We're going to take your car since it's already packed. Savage will take care of mine for me," he said.

She nodded and took Garret's car seat, getting him secured into the back seat. She shut the door and turned to find Razor holding out his hand. "Keys," he said.

Firefly rolled her eyes and handed them over to him. "I'm quite capable of driving," she challenged.

"Sure, but you just admitted that you were dog tired, so I'll drive, and you relax," he said. She wanted to "Aww," but from the look on his face, he wasn't in the mood for her to consider anything that he said to be cute. Instead, she opened the passenger side door and slipped into the car.

The drive to his house had her reliving their last night together; and just like that night, they drove most of the way in silence. "When we were back in the parking lot of the bar, what did you not say to me?" she asked.

"I'm not sure that I understand what you're asking me, honey," he said.

"I said that it was sad that Savage didn't know that his grandfather existed, and you looked like you were biting your tongue. What did you want to say to me?" she asked.

"I bit my tongue for a reason, Firefly. I'm not looking to start a fight. I just want to get us out of town before trouble comes looking for you," he admitted.

"That's not fair," she said. "Just say what you were going to say, Razor. I promise not to fight with you." That was a lie. She was just cranky and tired enough to start a fight with just about anyone who pissed her off.

"I was going to point out that our son wouldn't have known about me if you never landed in some trouble up in Boston. I'm just trying to figure out how Savage not knowing his grandfather was sad to you, but keeping our son from his father wasn't," he spat.

"It's not like that," she insisted. She was lying—he was completely right about the situation, but she wasn't sure how to defend herself. How could she? She should have tried harder to tell him about Garret, but instead, she ran away like a coward.

"Then tell me how it is, exactly," he said.

"I can't," she grumbled. "You're right, it is the same. I was going to keep our son from knowing his father. I tried to find you to tell you about him, but I didn't try hard enough. I should have told Savage about the pregnancy and then, maybe he would have helped me to track you down. I'm sorry, Razor. Seeing the two of you together now—I know that I shouldn't have kept him a secret. You both deserve to know each other and have a fresh start."

"Thank you for that, honey," he said. He reached across the console and pulled her hand onto his lap. "I appreciate your honesty and your apology. This is my fault too. If I wasn't so stubborn, I would have let you find me, and then, we wouldn't be in this mess. I've lost so much time with Garret, but I plan on making that up to him, starting now."

"I have to admit, when you walked into Savage's office, I saw thing going very differently. I was worried that you wouldn't believe that Garret is your son," she said.

Razor barked out his laugh, "Well, the kid looks just like me, so I won't be able to deny that he's mine."

Firefly giggled, "True," she agreed. "I thought that you might turn us away or be angry that I kept him from you, but you've been so kind and offered to help us. I just want you to know how much I appreciate your help, Razor," she said.

"To be honest, I am still a bit pissed that you kept him from me, but after hearing your story, I get it. You tried to find me, and I didn't make that easy on you. But you and I are going to have to make a pact if this is going to work out between us," he said.

"Wait, there's going to be an us?" she squeaked.

He shrugged, running his fingers over her palm. "If you want there to be, I'd like that, honey," he said. "But if all you came here for was me to protect Garret, tell me now. I want you both, Firefly. Can you give me that? Are you willing to try?"

That was quite a loaded question for her to have to answer right now. Involving Razor with her problems was one thing but inviting him into her life was quite another. Could she let him into her life? The tougher question was, could she let Razor into Garret's life?

"Yes," she whispered, "I'd like to try," she said. It was an honest answer. She had missed him like crazy after she left. The long nights, when Garret was asleep in his little crib, were the worst. She'd think about their night together and what she'd give to have another with him. But then, images of Razor with other women would fill her dreams and that was when she'd wake up hating herself for thinking about him at all.

"Good," he said. "I'd like to think of this part as our fresh start. You know, we can get to know each other and all the other stuff we skipped when we jumped into bed together," he offered.

"I'd like that, Razor," she admitted. He pulled into his driveway and opened the garage door, pulled into the two-car bay, and shut the door behind them. "I'm not taking any chances that someone hasn't followed you down here, honey," he said in way of explanation.

She looked into the back seat and found that Garrett was sound asleep. "He's finally sleeping. How about I sit out here with him, and you go on in and pack your things?" she asked.

"I'll be quick," he promised. He leaned over to gently brush his lips over hers and when he finished, she couldn't hide her goofy smile. "Stay put," he ordered. She watched as Razor disappeared into his house and looked back at her sleeping son once again.

"I'm so glad that you got to meet your daddy, Garret," she whispered. She was too. Razor seemed to be up for the challenge that she was throwing at him, and she had to admit, she was happy that he wanted to include her into the mix of things. She finally felt safe after so many weeks of having to look over her shoulder. Firefly just hoped like hell that she wasn't putting her son and Razor in harm's way. She'd never forgive herself if something happened to either of them.

RAZOR

By the time they got out to Ryder's hanger, poor little Garret was screaming his lungs out. "He's hungry," Firefly said. "I'm sorry, he only yells like this when he wants to nurse. Do you mind if I take a few minutes and fee him?" she asked.

"Of course," Razor agreed. "I'll meet with Ryder and fill him in on the itinerary while you feed him."

"Thanks," she said. He parked in the parking spot in front of the hanger and got out of her car. As soon as he lifted his son out of the car seat, he quieted. "You're really good with him," she breathed, taking the baby from him. Firefly lifted her top and as soon as Garret latched on, his crying completely stopped. Watching her feed their son felt natural to him, as though he hadn't missed the first year of his life.

"It's just beginner's luck," he said. "It looks like you're the one who's good with him, honey," he said. She sat back down in the passenger's seat, snuggling Garret as he ate. "I'll go check in with Ryder and be right back," he offered.

"All right," she agreed. "He usually eats for about fifteen minutes. I've got a few bananas that I'll give him on the plane to distract him. He loves those things."

"It seems that my son and I have that in common then," Razor said. "I love bananas too."

"Well, if you play your cards right, maybe he'll share with you," she teased.

Razor looked back into the hanger to see Ryder making his way out to them. "Be right back," he promised.

"Hey man," Ryder said, meeting him at the hanger doors. "Who did you bring with you?"

"You remember Firefly?" he asked.

"Yeah, but I didn't know her well. She left a while back, right?" Ryder asked.

"Yes," Razor breathed. "And now she's back with our son and well, she's in trouble."

"Wow," Ryder said. "Your son? Did you know about him?"

"No," Razor said. "Listen, it's a long story and we might be running out of time. She's feeding Garret now and then; we need to get loaded up and get in the air. Thanks for doing this, man," Razor said.

"Not a problem," Ryder agreed. "Anything for a brother. Where am I flying the three of you to?" he asked.

"West Virginia," Razor said.

"Ahh—Savage's cabin." Razor was surprised that Ryder

knew about the place, Savage didn't tell many people about his grandfather or his inheritance.

"He told you about that place?" Razor asked.

"Yeah," Ryder said. "I flew him and Bowie up to take a look at it after he found out that he had inherited it. It's a nice place," Ryder said. "A little rough around the edges, but not too bad."

"Suitable for a baby?" Razor asked. He was worried that he was taking Firefly and his son to a shack in the middle of the woods. "Tell me that there's at least electricity and indoor plumbing," he said.

Ryder chuckled. "Yes, it's fine for the baby and yes, it has both indoor plumbing and electricity. You guys will be just fine laying low out there." He hoped like hell that Ryder was right. He was going to have to figure out a way to get Firefly out of having to appear in court. It was the only way that he'd be able to keep her and Garret safe, and that was all he wanted to do right now.

"Just yell at me when the baby is done eating and we'll load up," Ryder said.

"Will do," Razor agreed.

The flight to West Virginia took just under two hours. Ryder had flown in as close as he could get to the cabin, but there was still an hour's drive to get out to the place. Garret had slept most of the flight and was still snoozing in his car seat when they put him into the SUV that Savage had waiting for them at the hanger. His Prez had thought of everything, and Razor was grateful for it.

"If you guys need anything, call my cell. I can be back here in a few hours and take you wherever you need to go," Ryder offered.

"Thanks, man," Razor said. "We appreciate everything you did for us. The ride here with a baby would have been brutal."

"I get it," Ryder said. "I have a few of my own and road trips with a baby are my least favorite thing to do."

Razor looked back to Firefly, "You ready to head out to the cabin?" he asked.

"I am," she agreed. "Garret's still sleeping, so we need to take advantage of the quiet while we have it."

Ryder chuckled, "Good luck guys," he said. "Keep us updated with what's going on." He helped them to load up the waiting SUV and they were heading out to Savage's cabin in no time.

Firefly was so quiet, that he wondered what was going on in her head. "What are you thinking?" he asked, reaching across the console to take her hand into his own.

"I guess I'm wondering if all this is necessary. I feel foolish that we have to run all the way to West Virginia to hide away from a mob family who may or may not be coming after me," she admitted.

"I get that," he said. "But with the messages that you said that they sent over the past few months, and the fact that

Razor's Edge

they not only know where you live but your apartment was ransacked, calls for us to take action."

"And our action is running?" she asked.

"Right now, yes," he breathed. "We're running to a secure place so that I can lock us down and keep you and Garret safe. Then, we need to come up with a plan to get you off of that case because there is no way that I'm going to let you anywhere near Francoli and the Manzoni family."

The GPS told them to take the next right and Razor pulled off the highway and started down a winding country road that felt like it went straight up to heaven. "The mountains in the state are for real," he said. "We're almost to Savage's cabin though," he said.

"I'm glad to hear that," she said. "I'm tired of traveling and I'm sure that Garret will be waking up soon for food. My boobs are killing me, and I really need to feed him." The last thing he needed to think about was her boobs. He was already thinking about all of the things he wanted to do to her once they got up to the cabin, but he'd have to wait his turn. Garret would always come first.

He pulled onto the little gravel path that could barely be considered a road. "We're almost there," he said. As if on cue, his son woke up and started screaming for his mother.

"That's good because we just ran out of time," she said.

"The GPS says we have to stay on this road for a mile and we'll be at the cabin," he said. "Talk about being off the beaten path. I wonder how Savage's grandfather lived out here with no one around."

"I don't know," Firefly breathed. "I think it sounds kind of nice—our own little secluded hideaway," she said. The thought of being hidden away with Firefly made him a bit anxious. Would she want him the way he wanted her? Razor knew that they had a lot of work to do to get back the trust that they lost after their first night together.

"I have to admit, I'm a little bit nervous about the three of us being hidden away up here," he whispered.

"Why?" she asked. "What are you worried about?"

"Crossing a line that we might not be ready to cross. I need to know that you're on board for everything this time—all of it, Firefly. I can't let you go again."

"I'm here for everything," she assured. "All of it."

"Will you sleep in my bed?" he asked.

"I'd like to, yes," she admitted, "if that's what you want."

"I want you in my bed, honey," he said. Garret was still crying in the back seat and Razor felt wrong about discussing wanting to sleep with his mother.

He pulled down to the cabin and realized that Savage and Ryder weren't kidding when they said the old place was rustic. "It's adorable," Firefly said.

"It's basically a shack," he said. "Although I have been promised that there is indoor plumbing and electricity in the cabin."

"Well, I don't care what condition it's in, I'm just thankful that we have a place to lay low until we can figure it all out," she said.

"I like the way that you call us a we," he said. "It makes me feel that you might stick around." Razor didn't want to get his hopes up that she'd stick around this time. Firefly could take off on him again, and that would hurt like hell, but he wanted to try with her.

"I'm not going anywhere, Razor," Firefly promised. "I know you have no reason to believe me, but I'm sticking around." She leaned over the console, their son still screaming from his car seat in the back and kissed his lips. Razor loved feeling her pressed up against him. Firefly felt right there against his body.

"Let's get in and you can get everything up and running while I feed our son," she ordered.

"Deal," he said. He walked around the SUV and opened the back door to smile at Garret. "Hey son," he whispered, trying to soothe the crying baby. "Mama's going to feed you now," he assured. He unbuckled his son's car seat and lifted him out of the backseat, patting his little back. Garret hiccupped and let out a few stray sobs as they walked to the cabin together. He handed the keys to the place to Firefly, and she struggled to get the deadbolt to turn. Razor handed Garret to her and finally jimmied the lock to open, pushing his way into the cabin.

"It just needs some WD40, and it will be as good as new," he assured. The place wasn't that bad on the inside. He could tell that Savage had done some updates, including a leather sectional that took up most of the family room and he even updated the appliances in the kitchen.

"I'll find the breaker and get the electric up and running," he said. "It will be getting dark soon enough." She nodded and settled on the sofa, changing Garret's diaper. He fussed the entire time until she started to feed him, and Razor thought it was pretty damn cute how much his son loved to eat but standing and watching Firefly feed his son wasn't going to get the cabin up and running.

He putzed around outside, finding the circuit breaker and turning it on. He got the electricity on and even made sure that they had hot water for bath time. He walked back into the cabin to find Firefly still feeding Garret and realized that it was a little chilly in the family room.

"I'll build a fire to take the chill off," he said.

"Thank you," she said. "I'm not used to having anyone helping me out. I got used to doing everything on my own."

"Well, I like helping out," he said. "In fact, I like taking care of you both," Razor said. "I'm glad that I have the chance to do that."

"Me too," Firefly said.

"How about I make us some dinner? I'll also make the bed and clean the bathroom—you know, get the tub ready for Garret's bath," Razor offered.

"Thank you," she said. "I brought a pack and play portable crib for him. I'm sure he's going to love not having to sleep in his car seat for a change. These past few days have been tough on him."

"I bet," Razor said. "Would you mind letting me give him a bath tonight? I mean, I have no idea what I'm doing, but you can talk me through it."

"That would be great," she said. "I'm sure Garret would love to have a new person to splash at night. I have to warn you, he likes to pee in the bath, so I usually try to hurry up and give him his bath before that happens."

"Right," Razor said. He felt as though he had so much to learn when it came to his son, he just hoped like hell that he'd catch up and find his way quickly.

FIREFLY

They finished cleaning up the dinner dishes together and when Garret started to get fussy, she filled the tub with warm, lavender bath water for him. Razor looked like a kid on Christmas, holding his naked son when he walked into the bathroom to give him his bath.

"I've never done this," he admitted.

"I'm sure that you'll be a natural," she said. "I mean, you've taken to fatherhood like a pro."

He smiled down at her, "Thanks for saying that, honey. It means a lot coming from the most fantastic mom I've ever met."

She giggled and shook her head at him. "Okay, stop stalling and get our son into the tub," she insisted.

He put Garret into the water and the baby squealed and kicked his little feet in the bubbles, soaking both of them as they sat on the edge of the tub. Razor laughed, distracting Garret from his kicking. "Sorry," she said. "He likes to splash in the tub. I should have warned you. I end up taking a bath after he's in bed, usually, because I feel like I'm already halfway there, so why not?"

He chuckled, "I think you might be right. How about you feed him when he's finished his bath and I'll get a bath ready for the two of us?" he offered, bobbing his eyebrows at her.

"You mean, the two of us? In the bathtub together," she added. "Will we fit?"

"Hell, you can sit on top of me, for all I care. I'd prefer it, really," he teased.

She giggled and slapped at his arm. "Do you think we're ready for this?" she asked.

"I don't know about you, but I'm ready for a bath. It's been a damn long day," he said.

"That's not what I meant," she insisted. "Are we ready for this next step? I know we have a kid and all, but we have some stuff to work through still, and jumping into bed—or the tub, in this case, might not be a good idea."

Razor leaned over and kissed her. "I'll follow your lead," he offered. "Take all the time you need. If you feel that this is too fast, we can wait. Just promise me that you'll spend the night in bed with me. I want to be near you, honey. I just got you back—both of you, and I don't want to let you go for now."

"Is that because you're worried that I'll run again?" she asked.

"No," he said. She could tell that she had hit a nerve and honestly, she had only herself to blame for him worrying about her taking off on him again. She was the one who left town and didn't tell him about his son.

"I won't leave again, Razor," she promised. "I won't run—you have my word."

Razor nodded, "Thank you for that, honey," he said. He turned to Garret who was watching their every move. "Now, let's get you all cleaned up, little man," he said. Garret squealed and clapped, making them both laugh. She didn't need time—she knew that she wanted him, and waiting was silly, given that they had a son together. Wanting Razor wouldn't go away. She knew that from spending almost two years apart from him. Her longing for him never dissipated, and she had a feeling that it never would.

"I'd like to have that bath with you, Razor," she said as he pulled Garret's wet, soapy body from the tub and wrapped him in a towel. "Let me take him and you get the bath ready for us. I'll be about twenty minutes."

"You're sure?" he asked.

"Very sure," she agreed. "But thank you for offering me time to think about what I want." She shrugged, "I want you, Razor. I have for a long time and that's not going to change."

"Good to know," he said. "I'll come to find you when the bath is ready," he offered.

"Thanks," she said. He kissed her and then kissed Garret's little head, making the baby giggle. She was going to quickly dress and feed her son, and then, she hoped to reconnect with the man who was slowly beginning to reclaim her heart. It was only right that he do the same with her body.

Garret was fussy and refused to go down, and Firefly was sure that Razor had probably given up and gone to sleep. She had put the baby in the crib and was patting his back when Razor came into the makeshift nursery to find her.

"He's super fussy tonight, I'm sorry," she whispered. "He's just about asleep now."

Razor kissed down the back of her neck to her shoulder. "You still want a bath?" he asked.

"Y-yes," she stuttered. "I'd like to have a bath with you, Razor." His hands felt as though they were everywhere, and she knew that if he kept touching her like he was, she would explode. It had been so long since anyone had touched her that way—two years in fact. Razor was the last man to claim her body and knowing just how good he was at doing so made her a little weak in the knees.

"I think he's asleep," Razor whispered into her ear. "I've got the bath ready, come with me," he ordered.

She followed him out of Garret's little room and down the hallway to the bathroom. Firefly felt nervous as hell, and she hated how her hands were shaking as she started to undress. "Here," Razor whispered, "let me." He grabbed the hem of her shirt from her hands, letting his fingers brush over hers, and tugged it up her body. Every inch that he uncovered of her made her shiver all the more.

"It's just me, honey," he breathed.

"I guess I'm just a bit nervous," she admitted. "I haven't been with anyone since we—well, you know since we were together. My body isn't the same as it was two years ago. Garret kind of changed me—in more ways than one. I have stretch marks now, too."

"I don't give a fuck about any of that, honey. Your body is perfect. You carried our son and to me, every stretch mark is sexy as fuck. You're amazing, honey," he assured.

"How do you do that?" she asked.

"Do what?"

"When I'm nervous as hell, you calm me with just one touch. When I think that I'm completely untouchable, you make me feel sexy. You're the one who's amazing, Razor," she said.

He didn't say anything—he didn't have to. She could see everything that he was feeling in his eyes. Razor was so intense, but when it was just the two of them, she felt it even more. He stared her down like she was his prey and honestly, Firefly would willingly let him capture her and do whatever he wanted to with her.

Razor had her completely naked in just minutes and the way he looked her over made her want to cover herself with her arms. Firefly wanted to hide, and he seemed to know it. "Don't," he ordered. "I want to see all of you, honey," he said.

"I want to see you too," she whispered. He was still fully

clothed and all she wanted was for him to strip bare and give her the same show that she was giving him.

"Let me help you into the tub," he offered, taking her hand. She sighed and stepped into the hot water, the bubbles from the lavender soaps that he used, pooling around her legs. He waited for her to settle into the water before he started to undress. Firefly couldn't take her eyes off of him, he was beautiful in a rustic sort of way. He didn't look like a lawyer out of the usual three-piece suits he wore. His upper body and arms were covered in tattoos and his overly long hair and beard were sure signs that he loved his MC world as much or more than he loved the lawyer world that he worked in.

"God, honey," he breathed. "When you look at me that way, I want to do every dirty thing you're thinking about in that pretty head of yours."

She smiled up at him. "Well, then, you should get into this tub with me, so that I can dirty you up, Razor." She slid forward and he climbed in behind her. She loved the way that they seemed to fit together as she slid back against his body. He was so much bigger than she was, but when they were like this, everything seemed to be in place—including her heart. Being with Razor felt right and even though that thought should have scared the hell out of her, it didn't.

His hands roamed over her body—seeming to be everywhere again and all she seemed capable of doing was moaning and writhing against him. Firefly loved the feel of his hard cock pressing into her ass as she practically sat on his lap. But that wasn't how she wanted him to take her. No, she wanted to be able to see him, to look into his eyes and see every promise that he would silently make her but not dare speak out loud.

She turned to straddle his lap, water sloshing up over the edge of the tub and onto the floor. "We're making a mess," she whispered against his lips.

He pushed her wet hair back from her face and kissed her. "Don't fucking care," he said between kisses. God, he was everything she remembered him to be and so much more.

She lowered herself onto his shaft, loving the way that he hissed out his breath as if it was almost too much for him to bear. "Baby," he breathed. "You feel so fucking good."

"You feel good too, Razor," she whispered. "What do you want me to do now?" she coyly asked.

"Ride me, honey," he ordered. Razor dug his fingers into her fleshy hipbones to help her slide up and down his shaft as if reminding her exactly how he liked it. She did exactly as he ordered, sliding up and down his cock, finding her release, shouting out his name. Firefly could feel his eyes on her, watching her enjoying her orgasm, and she should have felt the need to hide again, but she didn't. The way that he watched her was hot and she was sure that she'd never get enough of him looking at her like that.

He sucked her taut nipple into his warm mouth as he found his own release. He was beautiful to watch, and Firefly couldn't take her eyes off of him. How had she lived without this man for the past two years? The real question was when this was all over, would she be able to walk away from him again? Would she be able to live without Razor? She already knew the answers to her questions—she wouldn't be able to live without him in her life now. He'd ruined her for that possibility, and she wasn't one bit mad about it.

RAZOR

Razor needed to call in some favors if he was going to keep Firefly safe from the Manzoni family. He was going to have to come up with a reason to keep her from the case and he knew just who to call to help him out.

He pulled up his list of judges and found Judge Josephs' number. He called her office and asked to speak with her, telling her assistant that it was in reference to Penny Quinn. The judge had a soft spot for Firefly. Hell, she had even lied to him about where she was. She kept Firefly's secret about the baby. If anyone could help her, it was Judge Josephs.

"Hello," the judge answered.

"Hi Judge Josephs, this is Garret Tracey," he said.

"What can I do for you Mr. Tracey?" she asked.

"It's not what you can do for me, it's what you can do for

Penny Quinn," he said. Firefly walked into the room, and he asked the judge to hold on, cupping his hand over the phone.

"Who are you talking to?" she asked.

"Judge Josephs," he said.

She gasped, "Why did you involve her in this mess?" she asked.

"Because I think that she can help you, Firefly. I think that she might be one of the only people who can help you out of this mess," Razor said.

"Fine, put her on speaker," she insisted.

He nodded, "Judge, I have Penny here with me now, I'm going to put you on speaker if that's all right with you."

"Fine," she said. He could tell that the judge still didn't completely believe him, and why should she? Firefly had convinced her that he wasn't a good guy. It was how she had gotten the judge to keep her secret about the baby and her whereabouts.

"Hello, Judge Josephs," Firefly whispered.

"Penny," she breathed into the other end of the call. "I'm so glad to hear from you. Are you all right?"

"Yes," she said. "I'm with Razor, so I'm fine," she said.

"How do I know that you're truly safe?" the judge asked.

"Remember the last time that we saw each other? I told you that I was pregnant, and that the baby's father wasn't a nice guy?" she asked. Hearing Firefly say those words felt like a knife to the gut.

"Of course," the judge said. "I was so worried about you

and then, Mr. Tracey came looking for you, so I assumed that he was the man you were speaking of."

"He was, but I lied to you. I told you that so that you'd keep my secret. I knew that sooner or later, someone would come looking for me and if you thought that they meant me harm, you wouldn't tell them where I was or that I was pregnant."

"Smart girl," the judge praised. "Although I don't like that you lied to me."

"I know, and I'm sorry," Firefly said. "I was desperate and didn't know what to do at the time. I thought that running away was my only option, but I was so wrong."

"Where did you go?" the judge asked.

"To Boston," Firefly said. "I took the bar and passed it before my son was born, and as soon as I could find a good daycare for him, I found a job at a decent firm up there."

"That's wonderful," the judge said. "But I'm guessing that you aren't calling to tell me how well things are going for you. I have to admit, I overheard Mr. Tracey tell you that I might be the only person who can help you. What's happened?" she asked.

"Things were going well for a while. I took on more and more cases and worked my way up in the firm," Firefly recounted. "I thought that I was well on my way to my dreams of making partner someday and then, I got hit with a case that might destroy it all for me."

"That's awful," the judge said. "Is it a high-profile case?" she asked.

"You could say that," Firefly admitted. "I am supposed to represent Marcos Francoli. He's a part of the Manzoni family and I've been receiving threatening notes since I was assigned his case."

The judge gasped, "I've heard of the Manzoni family," she said. "They have a far reach, and I'm betting that they don't want you messing this up for Mr. Francoli."

"Right," Firefly agreed. "That's the gist of what the notes said. But they added in that if I did mess things up for him, my son and I would pay the price."

"Tell me that you went to the authorities," the judge ordered.

"Not at first," she said. "I went to my boss, and he told me to ignore the messages, but then, they started to get delivered to my house, and knowing that they knew where Garret and I lived scared the heck out of me."

"I'm sure that it did," the judge agreed.

"I came home from work one day and found that my apartment had been broken into and that's when I went to the cops, but they did nothing to help me. They wrote up an incident report and told me that they'd contact me if they had any further questions or leads."

"Do you think that your boss and the police up in Boston might be on the Manzoni's payroll?" the judge asked.

"At first, I didn't want to believe it, but now, I do," Firefly admitted. "I didn't feel safe staying up in Boston, so I did the only thing that I could think to do. I went home to Huntsville and found Razor," she said. "I told him about the baby, and he's been helping me."

"Are you in Huntsville now?" the judge asked.

"No," Razor breathed. There was no way that he'd tell anyone besides Savage and Ryder where they were laying low. He wouldn't take any chances with her or Garret. "I have Firefly and our son in a safe location. Only two other people know where we are, and I trust them with our lives."

"Of course," the judge said. "How can I help?"

"We need to get Firefly removed from the case. She's tried to recuse herself from representing Francoli but hasn't had any luck. It wouldn't surprise me if he's paid off the judge on his case too. Firefly has evidence that Francoli is guilty. She even has video footage on a thumb drive that she has been able to keep hidden. We need for that to get into the right hands, but we're not sure who that might be. We need her off this case."

"Let me do some digging. I have a few friends up in that area who own firms and might be willing to give me a hand. Will you trust me to keep your secret and discreetly ask around on your behalf?" the judge asked.

"Of course," Firefly agreed. "Thank you so much for doing this, Judge Josephs."

"You are welcome," the judge said. She asked Firefly a few more questions about the case, making sure that she had all of the necessary details, and made the promise to be in touch very soon. He ended the call and tossed his cell to the kitchen table.

"Thank you," Firefly whispered.

"For what?" Razor asked.

"For helping me. I sometimes get in my own way by not wanting to ask anyone for help. Thank you for taking charge and calling the judge. I probably wouldn't have called her for help, but you're right, we need to keep Garret safe. If she can help, then I'll finally be free of this mess, and we can get on with our lives." Hearing her say that she was going to get on with her life made him feel a bit queasy. Did she mean that they could move forward together or separately? He was foolish to believe that her sleeping in his bed and making love to him constituted her wanting to spend her life with him, but that's what had happened.

"Why do you look angry, Razor?" she asked. Firefly smoothed her hand down his face and cupped his cheek. He couldn't help but lean into her caress. Every time she touched him felt like he was finding his way back home after being gone for a damn long time.

"I'm not angry," he breathed. "Just worried."

"What are you worried about?" she asked.

"I'm worried that when you say that you're going to get on with your life, you mean without me. I don't know what to expect here, honey," he admitted.

She smiled up at him, going up on her tiptoes to gently kiss his lips. "I'd like it if you got on with your life too, Razor—with Garret and me. I like being with you," she said.

Razor let out the pent-up breath that he didn't know that he was holding. "I like being with you too, honey," he said.

"Good," she whispered, kissing him again. "I can't tell you where this all ends up, Razor, but I'd like for us to find out together. I just feel like my life is so up in the air right now, that I can't make you promises that I won't be able to keep. But one promise that I can make to you is that when this is all over, I want to be with you. I'm not here with you now just because you've promised to keep us safe. That might have been how this all started, but I don't feel that same way now."

"Thank fuck," he growled. "Because I don't feel that way either. I didn't offer to keep you two safe because I felt obligated to. I mean, sure, Garret's my son, but I offered to help you because I still had feelings for you, Firefly. I guess that makes me a giant sap, but I don't give a shit. I want both you and Garret to be a part of my life. I want to make you promises, but I won't until you're ready to hear them."

"Thank you for that, Razor," she whispered. He lifted her into his arms, and she squealed. "What are you doing?" she asked.

"I'm taking advantage of our son's nap time. How about I make you one promise right now?" he asked.

"Oh—what's that?" she asked, wrapping her arms around his neck. He started to the back of the cabin, where their bedroom was.

"How about I promise to make you scream out my name over and over again until you can't scream anymore?" he asked.

She giggled, "I think that might mess up your plan to take

advantage of me while our son is sleeping," she teased. "But I'm all for trying things your way," she agreed. He picked up his pace, practically running with her back to the bedroom and tossing her onto the bed. "How long do you think we have?" he asked.

She looked over at the clock that sat on the bedside table. "Maybe an hour—if we're lucky," she said.

"Well, then, start taking off your clothes, honey. I don't want to waste a second," he ordered. He loved watching her strip out of her jeans and t-shirt. She wasn't wearing a bra and seeing her in just her skimpy, lacy panties made him hard.

He had watched her strip and forgot to take off his own clothes. She looked him over, gifting him with her shy smile. "If you plan on using every second to your advantage, you better hurry up and catch up with me, Razor," she demanded. He'd never moved so quickly in his life. "Now who's eager?" she teased. He laughed as he climbed up her body, covering hers with his own.

"I want you to be on top," he said, rolling over with her, and putting her on top of him. "I like to watch you when you ride my cock and come for me," he said. He loved the little moan that escaped her parted lips as she slid onto his shaft. Razor couldn't get enough of her, no matter how many times he took her, he still wanted more.

"You feel so good," she moaned, seating herself on his cock.

"You do too, baby," he groaned. "Ride me, Firefly." He let

his hands roam her beautiful body, playfully plucking her taut nipples, loving the way her wet folds slid over his erection.

Firefly road him, and every time she cried out his name, he worried that she was going to wake Garret. She smiled down at him, and he knew that she was going to give as good as she got.

"Your turn," she whispered against his lips. "I want to hear you call out my name, this time." If she only knew that he'd do anything that she'd ask him to do for her, she'd realize just how much power she held over him.

Firefly wiggled her hips, riding him just the way she knew that he liked it and when he came, he shouted out her name, knowing that they'd wake the baby for sure this time, but he didn't care. She rode his shaft, milking his cock until he was completely sated, and then, collapsed on top of his chest.

"Wow," he breathed, running his hand down her back.

"Wow doesn't even begin to cover it, Razor. I don't know if I'm crazy or what, but every time we're together, I feel like I'm right where I'm supposed to be." He cupped her ass and hummed his approval, not sure that he was ready to give her the words yet.

"I feel the same way," he croaked, his voice still hoarse from shouting out her name.

As if on cue, their son started crying from his room and she stood. "I'll go grab him," she said. He watched as Firefly disappeared from their room and he was sure that she was perfect. Now, all he had to do was convince her to be his because that was all he wanted—promises be damned because he wanted to make her every fucking promise that he could think of.

FIREFLY

Firefly wasn't sure if she was being completely naive, or if calling her boss was a good idea, but she was going to at least try to reason with him about getting out of the case.

She found her cell phone in her purse and turned it on. Razor had warned her about leaving it on, and people possibly being able to track her. She was careful about turning off the location locator on her phone, but she couldn't be too careful, so she usually left it off.

"Hey, what are you doing?" Razor asked.

"I'm getting up my nerve to call my boss," Firefly admitted. "I hate that I'm this nervous about talking to him. I'm just worried that he's going to use my not showing up to court to fire me."

"Maybe, if his firm didn't put you on a case like this, he

wouldn't have to worry about you showing up to court," Razor said. "Your boss should have had your back when you went to him and told him that you were receiving threatening messages."

"You're right," she agreed. "But right now, I'm focused on protecting my son and hopefully keeping my job. I worked hard to get to where I am."

"I know that you did, but some things just aren't worth the fight honey," he said. She knew that he was right and that she was being foolish. Once this mess was over, she planned on moving back home to Alabama so that her son could grow up knowing his father. She was hoping that Razor would be good with her plan, but just in case, she needed a plan B. She was going to hold onto her job until she knew that she didn't need it anymore and that would involve her landing a job back in Huntsville, to move back home to.

"I think that I at least owe Bill a call," she said. "I need to let him know that I won't be in anytime soon."

Razor sighed, "Fine, just put the call on speaker so that I can listen in. Don't give him any details and if I think he's tracing the call, I'm going to tell you to hang up. Got it?"

"Got it," she agreed. She found his contact information and dialed his number. Bill answered on the first ring. "Is it really you, Penny?" he asked.

"Yes," Firefly said. "It's me."

"Oh, thank God," he breathed into the other end of the call. "I was so worried. Are you back in town?"

"Um, no," she said.

"Why the hell not? Penny, you are supposed to show up to court in just days now. You can't miss your court date, or you will be found in contempt. Mr. Francoli has made it very clear; he wants you to represent him and no one else. He won't settle for you not showing up, Penny. He'll push the issue."

"I don't care if he pushes the issue. He wants me on his case because he wants to control me. He knows that I can prove him guilty, and that's why I've been receiving threatening notes and why my apartment was broken into. The Manzoni family went there looking for my evidence."

"Evidence?" he asked. "What evidence do you have?"

"I have a flash drive with footage of Francoli beating that poor man to death. He left him there to die and he knows that I found the footage from the security cameras in that warehouse. The family won't leave me alone until I'm dead and can't tell the truth anymore. They'll kill my son too, and I won't let that happen." She looked over at Razor and he looked mad enough to spit nails. Firefly worried that he was about to end their call, but she had a hunch that her boss knew something that he wasn't sharing yet. She hoped that with a bit more pushing, she'd be able to get him to talk.

"Where is the flash drive now?" Bill asked.

"In a safe place," she said.

"Did you hide it in your apartment?" he questioned.

"No," she said. "I'm not an idiot, Bill."

"So, you have it with you then?" he guessed. She wasn't

about to tell him that either. When she didn't answer, he took that as his cue that he had guessed correctly. "Where are you? I'll come to get the hard drive and turn it over to the proper authorities," he assured. She was sure that by proper authorities, he meant that he'd turn it over to the Manzoni family because she was pretty sure that they were paying him off too.

"I don't think that's a good idea," she said. "I'll keep it for safekeeping. What I need for you to do is find another lawyer to take the case because I won't be able to. I'm taking a leave of absence until this is over and I know that my son and I are safe."

Bill barked out his laugh. "You'll never be safe, Penny," he spat. "They won't stop looking for you."

"By they, you mean the Manzoni family, right Bill?" she asked.

"What?" he asked. "The Manzoni family won't stop as long as you have that drive, and I won't put my neck on the line for you. I'll tell them where to find you before I put my life on the line. If you don't show up, you'll be in contempt, and they will put more men on their mission of trying to find you. I'm just trying to help you out here, honey."

Razor's growl filled the bedroom, and he pulled the phone from her hand. "She's not your honey," Razor shouted. "You threatening her isn't going to work either. It doesn't matter who's coming for us—they will never touch our son or Penny," he said. "How about you run back to the Manzoni family to let them know that they can't touch her—now or ever."

"Who is this?" Bill asked. "Penny are you all right?" She tried to take the phone back from Razor and he ended the call, tossing it onto the bed.

"What the hell was that?" she asked.

"He's working for the Manzoni family—you heard him," Razor defended.

"We can't know that for sure," she said. "I was trying to get him to confess."

"He was tracing your call, honey," Razor said. She knew that he was probably right, but she was still pissed that he took over her phone call. "I'm just trying to keep you safe, Firefly," he said. "You and Garret, and that man wants to hurt you both."

"Fine," she said. "But if you just lost me my job, you're going to have to hire me at your firm," she teased.

"Done," he agreed. She gasped as he walked past her, slapping her ass on the way out of the room. Did he really just hire her?

"What the hell just happened?" she breathed to herself. She had been asking that question a lot today and Firefly knew that it had everything to do with the hot a sin lawyer who just walked out of the bedroom.

It took two weeks for the judge to call her back. She thought that waiting for her due date with Garret was excruciating but waiting for the judge to call was worse. She answered her phone, and the judge didn't give her time to exchange pleasantries.

"Resign," she almost shouted into the other end of the phone.

"I'm sorry," Firefly said, pretending not to understand her. "Did you just tell me to resign from the firm that I work for?"

"Yes, I did," the judge confirmed. "I did some digging around and I'm almost positive that your boss is being paid by the Manzoni family, Penny," she said. "You'll never win the fight if that's the case. If you quit, the firm will be forced to find a replacement for you and I'm betting that your boss will be put up for the task. If he already works for the Manzoni family, they won't take any more chances with a novice lawyer trying to cut their teeth on their first big case. They will demand one of the firm's top lawyers. That's when you anonymously turn over the flash drive that you have with your evidence, to the opposing team of lawyers. How did you come to have that in your possession?" Judge Josephs asked.

"I'm not sure that I should answer that question, Judge," she admitted. "Let's just say that it might not hold up in court."

"Well, that won't be your problem anymore, not once you

turn it over," the judge said. "You don't seem very surprised that your boss is involved with this mob family, Penny."

"I'm not," she admitted. "I called to talk to Bill shortly after we spoke. I told him that I couldn't get back in time to handle the case and that I was taking some personal time with my son. That's when he informed me that wasn't an option. He said that if I didn't return in time for court, I'd be found in contempt and he'd make sure that a warrant would be issued for my arrest."

"Well, that's not very nice now, is it?" the judge asked.

"No," Firefly agreed, "it's not. I asked him why he was being so nasty, and he told me that he wouldn't risk his own neck to save me or my kid. He said that the Manzoni family would find me and make good on their threats, and when I challenged him and asked him why, he said that he would see to it personally that they find out where I'm staying."

"Please tell me that was an empty threat and that he's not one of the people you trusted with your secret," the judge said.

"He doesn't know where I am," she assured.

"Good," Judge Josephs said, "how did you leave it with him?"

"Well, I didn't leave anything with Bill. You see, my overly protective security detail was listening in since I had the call on speaker, and Razor informed my boss that he wouldn't let him or anyone else get near me."

"You see, I knew I liked Mr. Tracey," the judge said. "I'm assuming that he's listening into our conversation now."

"I am, Judge," Razor said.

"I think that your security detail is spot on, Penny," she said. "How about you send over a letter of resignation to your boss, letting him know that you quit, effective immediately. He'll have no choice but to step in to find your replacement."

"That won't stop the Manzoni family from coming after her," Razor said. "She knows too much, and they won't let her live with the information that she has on them."

"They know about the flash drive then?" the judge asked.

"I believe that they do. I think that's why they broke into my apartment and ransacked it. They were looking for something, but they never stood a chance of finding it. I didn't leave it in my apartment. I told my boss what had happened and that I had hidden it someplace that they'd never look. He asked me where that was, but I was already getting red flags from the guy, so I lied and told him that I had a security deposit box at a bank downtown."

"You sent him on a wild goose chase?" Razor asked.

"I did," she said. "He texted me after our conversation and I knew that he wasn't going to give up until I gave him some sort of answer, so I lied."

"Well, it won't be long before they come looking for it and if you have it with you, they will stop at nothing to find you," the judge said.

"I know," she said. "Your plan gets me off the case, but I still have the threats from the Manzoni family to worry about."

"If we can prove that Mr. Francoli is guilty and that he's linked to the Manzoni family, they might have bigger problems to worry about than you," the judge said.

"She's right," Razor agreed. "One problem at a time. The last thing we need is an arrest warrant going out for you because you failed to show up for court. We're cutting it close, but if you resign now, effective immediately, you might just be able to get out of having to represent Francoli. Then, we'll make sure that the files end up in the right hands. Can we trust the other side's lawyers?" he asked the judge.

"From what I've gathered, yes," the judge said. "I believe that you can."

"All right," Razor agreed. "We'll make sure that they get the files to take down Francoli and link him to the Manzoni family. We'll figure things out from there. Thanks, Judge," he said.

"My pleasure," Judge Josephs said. "Keep me updated," she ordered.

"We will, Judge," Firefly agreed. "Thank you." They ended the call, and she crossed the kitchen to get Garret out of his highchair. He had been eating his cheerios and was so quiet, she forgot that he was in the room with them.

"I wonder how much this will affect him," she whispered, snuggling him close to her as he squirmed to get back into his seat. Her son had a one-track mind when it came to food. "Do you think that he will remember any of this?" she asked.

Razor crossed the room to take him from her and Garret reached for his father, smiling up at him as if he was the best thing he'd ever seen. "No," he said. "I don't think that he'll remember any of this. He's resilient. Look how quickly he's accepted me being around."

"He seemed to take to you the moment he saw you," she reminded. "He fell asleep in your arms the first time you help him. Babies don't usually do that at this age," she insisted. "You two seem to have a bond that even I can't explain."

He kissed the top of their son's head and she smiled as Garret snuggled into Razor's big body, as if proving her point for her. "See," she breathed. "He was just squirming around for me to put him back in his seat to eat the rest of his cereal. But with you, he calms right down and behaves."

"You seem upset by that, honey," Razor assessed.

"Not so much upset, but it's very unexpected. I mean, I've been with him his whole life. He came out from inside of me, and he fights me at every turn. I change his diaper and he throws a fit. I give him a bath and he screams bloody murder. The only time he likes me is when I put one of my boobs in his mouth."

Razor smiled at her and nodded. "I like you when you put your boobs in my mouth too, honey," he teased.

She giggled and shook her head at him. "You know what I mean, Razor. I'm just a milk truck for him."

He pulled her into his body, and she snuggled in next to their son who was drifting off to sleep on Razor's chest. "That's just not true," he said. "You're everything to Garret. You kept him safe inside of you until it was time for him to be born. You fed him and made sure that he was growing.

He's the happiest kid that I've ever met and that's all because of you," Razor said. She needed to hear that from him. So often, she felt like a complete failure as a mother, she needed to hear that the man she adored thought that she had done a good job with their son. "You're a fantastic mom," he added.

"Thank you for saying all of that," she whispered, stroking back a strand of soft, strawberry-blond hair from her son's forehead. "I needed to hear it."

"I meant every word," Razor said.

"I guess I'm rethinking every move that I ever made, you know? From the time that I found out that I was pregnant to the part where I ran out of town, not telling you about your son. I wish that I could go back in time and change so much of what's happened. If I would have just stuck around and been brave enough to face you and tell you about him, I would have never gone to Boston, and I wouldn't be in this mess now. We'd all be safe at home, in Huntsville." It was her biggest regret—running away, and now, she realized how much would be different if she'd only rethought her decision to hide from him.

"I don't care about any of that. Nothing can be changed from our past. You don't think that there are aspects that I'd like to go back in time and fix. I've already told you that I acted like a coward and hid away from you. If I would have found you and demanded more than just one night with you, you wouldn't have felt the need to run from me. But we can't change any of it, so why stand here and play the what-if game? Let's just find our way out of this mess and then, we can decide what will be. That game is a lot more fun to play, honey," he said.

He was right. Playing the what will be game would be so much more fun. She just hoped that her future involved him because losing Razor now would kill her. She'd run from him once, but Firefly knew that running from him again would be impossible. Her heart just wouldn't allow it.

RAZOR

Firefly's phone was ringing, and Razor found it on her bedside table. "Babe, your phone is ringing," he said. "I thought that you had it turned off."

"I did but I tried to call Judge Josephs and I guess I forgot to turn it back off. Can you answer it for me? I'm changing Garret's diaper," she yelled from the next room.

"Sure," he agreed. He noticed that the caller ID said, "Unknown caller" and he was a bit leery of answering the phone. "Hello," he answered.

"Hi, I'm trying to reach Miss Penny Quinn," a man said.

"Can I tell her who's calling?" Razor asked.

"This is Dr. Franklin at Huntsville General Hospital. I'm calling in reference to Judge Josephs. She is in our care here and has asked me to reach out to Miss Quinn."

"Um, hold just a moment, please," Razor said. He walked

into the little nursery that they had made for Garret and found Firefly. "The hospital back home is calling they said that Judge Josephs is in the hospital, and she's asked them to call you."

"Oh God," she breathed, taking the phone from him. "Is she all right?"

"Not sure," he said. "The doctor's name is Dr. Franklin."

She nodded, putting the call on speaker. "This is Penny Quinn," she said.

"Hello Miss Quinn," the doctor said. "Judge Josephs has been admitted into my care here at Huntsville General."

"What happened?" Firefly asked.

"She was at the courthouse working late Monday evening, and apparently, she was attacked on her way to her car, in the parking lot," the doctor said.

"Will she be okay?" Firefly asked.

"She's stable for now," the doctor said. "When she was brought in, things were touch and go. She was stabbed five times, but we've managed to stabilize her and I'm hoping that she will make a full recovery."

"May I speak with her?" Firefly asked.

"She's been sedated for her comfort. She woke briefly this morning and asked me to call you, but she was very agitated. We had to sedate her again. I can have her call you once she's able to talk," he offered.

"Would I be allowed in to see her?" she asked.

"Firefly," Razor growled. She shushed him and he wanted to take the phone away from her, but he knew that would do no good. The determination that he saw in her eyes told him that she wouldn't back down from him.

"I'm sure that can be arranged," the doctor assured. Razor felt sick just thinking about Firefly running home to see the judge. She'd be putting herself in danger and that would never fly with him.

She thanked the doctor and ended the call, after getting his information to check in with him later. "You're not going back to Huntsville, Firefly, so just put that out of your head," he insisted.

"You can't tell me that I'm not allowed to go home to see the judge. She was one of the only people to believe in me. She gave me a chance when most people would have tossed me away." He wanted to point out that he felt the same way about her, but he didn't. He'd fight one battle at a time with her.

"I know that honey, but do you honestly believe that she'd want you to put yourself into danger by running back to town?" he asked. He was going to try to appeal to her on any level necessary. Right now, he'd try to reason with her, but he was willing to throw her over his shoulder and lock her in a fucking closet if necessary.

"I won't be in danger," she promised. "I'll slip in and back out before anyone even knows that I'm there."

"What about Garret?" he asked.

"You can keep him here, with you. He'll be safe and I'll be back before you know it," she said.

"No fucking way," he breathed. "There is no way that I'm

letting you go back to Alabama by yourself. Hell, they found the judge and stabbed her five times. What do you think they'll do to you? They probably went after her to get to you, honey," he said. "Have you thought about that?"

"I have, but as I said, I'll slip in and out before they even know it," she assured.

"They aren't novices, Firefly. They're probably watching the room where she's being kept. Does she even have a security detail?" he asked.

"If a judge was attacked on county property, the authorities will have her under surveillance," Firefly said.

"I'm going to ask Savage to send over a couple of guys to keep an eye on her," Razor said. "And if you won't let go of heading south to see her, I'm going with you. The three of us will go, and you and Garret won't leave my sight—got it?" he asked.

She squealed and clapped her hands. "Thank you," she gushed. "Besides you and Garret, the judge is the closest thing that I have to family. I need to make sure that she's safe and has everything that she needs," she said.

"I get it," he said. "But I won't compromise your or Garret's safety for you to see her, honey."

"I promise that you won't have to," she said.

"I'll call Ryder and see if he can fly us down," he said.

"Will we stay in Huntsville?" she asked.

"Probably not," he said. "This will be a quick trip. If they found the judge, then they are looking for you. We just need to make sure that they won't be able to find us."

Ryder showed up at the hanger early the next morning. He had texted Razor to meet him out there at seven and that meant a very early morning for the three of them, but Garret was the only one who didn't seem to mind. He and Firefly were feeling a little worse for wear though.

They found Ryder in the plane, getting ready for the return trip. "Hey," Razor said. He had Garret in his little car seat and Ryder peeked in at his sleeping son.

"He's asleep every time I see him," Ryder said. "He's so cute—good thing he looks just like his mother."

"Shut up," Razor grumbled.

"You look beat, man," Ryder said.

"I am and so is Firefly. I don't think that she slept at all last night; she was so worried about the judge," Razor said. "Poor thing tossed and turned all night."

"I'm sorry to hear that, but maybe this quick trip home will help," Ryder said.

"We appreciate it and I want you to bill me, not Savage for all of this back and forth," Razor said. Firefly climbed onto the plane and handed Razor the baby's diaper bag.

"Hey, Ryder," she said.

"Hi Firefly," Ryder said. He turned back to Razor, "We'll settle up later," Ryder offered. "For now, how about we just make sure to get you both in and out of there safely," he offered.

"Thanks," Razor said.

"Any news about the judge since last night?" Firefly asked.

"I haven't heard anything new. The last time I talked to Savage, he sent over two of our guys to help guard her room. The doctor in charge of her case wasn't thrilled that we barged into the hospital and kind of took over, but you know the guys in the club, that's just how we do things," Ryder said.

Firefly giggled, "I'm familiar with the way you all do things," she teased, looking up at Razor.

"Hey," Razor said. "I won't apologize for taking care of you and our son, honey," he said.

"I wouldn't want you to apologize for any of it, Razor," she said. "I wouldn't want you any other way." She went up on her tiptoes and gently kissed his cheek.

Ryder cleared his throat, "We should be back home in a couple of hours. Savage has a car waiting for you at my hanger and you'll go directly to the hospital and go in through the back. One of the guys is waiting there for you and will help you get up to the judge's room. You will have twenty to thirty minutes to visit and then, it will be time to go. Do not leave the judge's room, not even to go to the bathroom. After that, you will be escorted back to your vehicle and will drive directly back to the hanger where I'll be waiting to reload you three into the plane and we'll take off and head back to West Virginia."

"Wow," Razor said, "you guys have thought of everything," he said.

"That's all Savage's doing. I'm just relaying the orders and flying the plane," he said. "You have to understand, Firefly, if the judge isn't awake still, there will be no way to spend more time with her. You'll have to be happy with just seeing her."

"I understand," Firefly said. "I just want to see her and to tell her how much I appreciate everything that she's done for me and Garret."

"You'll get the chance to do that," Razor promised. "But we agree to stick to the rules. No one will even know we're there."

"Great, let's hit the road," Ryder ordered. "I'm sure that you guys are anxious to get back home."

"We are," Razor said. "Even if it's for just a short time. It will be nice to be home."

FIREFLY

Firefly grew more anxious with every passing mile to the hospital. Razor didn't let go of her hand the whole time as if he could sense her mood. "You okay?" he asked.

"I will be," she lied. "I just want to see her, but I hope that I'm not making a huge mistake by demanding that I get to see her. I'd never want to put you or Garret into danger," she said.

"I know that," Razor said. "With all of the guys helping out, I don't think we'll have much to worry about. You just concentrate on your visit with the judge and the guys, and I will keep you and Garret safe," he promised. She knew that she was asking a lot by demanding that she go home to see Judge Josephs, but the woman was like family to her, and not going back to see her felt wrong.

Razor parked in the back parking lot, just like Ryder told

him to do, and Savage's husband, Bowie was waiting for them just inside the door. He let them in and took Garret's car seat from Razor. "As long as you're both cool with it, I can babysit and keep him safe while you have your visit," he offered.

She looked up at Razor and he nodded. "Bowie, Savage, and Dallas have a bunch of kids," he said. "Garret will be safe with Bowie."

"There's a bottle and some snacks in the diaper bag," she said, handing it to Bowie. "He might also need a change." She made a face and he chuckled.

"I can handle a poopy diaper, Firefly," he assured. "Just go and visit the judge. Your time started when you walked in the back door. I'll meet you back here in twenty minutes."

Razor checked his watch and nodded. "We'll be back in twenty. Take care of him," he said, nodding to his son.

"I won't let him out of my sight," Bowie promised. Firefly peeked in at her son, almost not sure if leaving him was a good idea or not, but she had already come all this way, not seeing the judge wasn't an option.

Razor grabbed her hand and led her to the back stairs. "She's on the third floor," he said. "We can't take the chance of being seen by taking the elevators, sorry," he said.

"Not a problem," she said. "After traveling all day, I could use some cardio." They practically ran up the three flights of steps and when they got up to the third floor, Razor just about shoved her body behind his own.

"Stay behind me and do as I say," he ordered. He led her

into the judge's room, nodding to two guys who were standing outside of her door. Both were wearing leather vests with their MC patches. Firefly had to admit, having them there to help keep an eye on the judge gave her some peace. It was comforting knowing that if whoever did this to her decided to come back to finish the job, he'd meet with some resistance.

Firefly walked through the door expecting to find the judge still unconscious but was happily surprised to find her sitting, sipping some water that a nurse was helping her with. Her face was bruised. Dark black and blue blotches covered her face, and her left arm was cast and in a sling.

"You're awake," Firefly whispered.

"She just woke up a few hours ago," the nurse explained. "You can have a short visit, but Judge Josephs needs her rest."

"I'll be fine," the judge insisted. "Can you give us a few minutes? I have some things that I need to tell Penny and would prefer privacy."

"Of course," the nurse agreed. "You know how to reach me if you need anything."

The judge nodded, "Little red button," she said, nodding to her bedside. She waited for the nurse to disappear from the room and pointed to the chairs next to her bedside. Firefly and Razor took the hint, and both sat.

"You two took quite a chance coming back here," she whispered. "Although I am happy to see you both, you can't stay. You aren't safe here."

"We know," Razor said. "I tried to convince Firefly that

this wasn't a good idea, but she had other plans. There was no way that she'd stay away."

"You can read me the whole, 'I told you so' riot later," Firefly said. "Right now, I want to know exactly what happened to you, Judge," she insisted.

The judge took another sip of her water and put it back on the little bedside table that they had hovering over her lap. "I was heading home from work and a man jumped me. He asked me where you were. He said that you had something that his boss wanted and that he'd do what he had to do in order to get it from you. I now understand that what he meant by that was that he'd beat me black and blue and break a few bones while he was at it."

"I'm so sorry," Firefly sobbed. Razor wrapped an arm around her shoulder and the judge reached for her hand.

"It's not your fault," Judge Josephs assured. "I was someone that they thought that they could use to get to you, Penny."

"I just wish that there is something that I can do to make this all go away. If I had just stayed in town and hadn't run, none of this would have happened. I would have never gotten involved in this case and you wouldn't be laying here in a hospital bed now," Firefly said.

"Nonsense," the judge said. "You followed your own path and became a lawyer, just as you always wanted. Things turned out the way that they were supposed to. I do have another message for you. The man who attacked me said that the Manzoni family gives their word that they will walk away from you both if you turn over the evidence that you have on Marcos Francoli to them."

She looked over at Razor and she shook his head. "We can't take their word for it, honey," he said. "If you turn over the flash drive to them, they'll still come for us. You could still put Francoli away if you testify against him. You know what's on the thumb drive and they won't just let you live with that knowledge."

"He's right," the judge agreed. "I'm afraid that I don't trust them at their word either. I think that you should turn the thumb drive over to the authorities," she said. "Does the evidence on it link Francoli to the Manzoni family?" she asked.

"Yes, it does," Firefly said. "There will be no question that he's guilty and that he's working for the Manzoni family. But doing that will put everyone in my life in danger."

"I can make sure that doesn't happen," the judge assured. "I have connections and can get you involved in a witness protection program until this can all be worked out."

"I'd have to hide away again?" Firefly asked. She felt as though they had done nothing but hide away over the past couple of months. While she loved spending time with Razor, reconnecting with him, and watching him get to know his son, she was ready to go back home. The question was, where she considered home now. It used to be Alabama and she'd love for that to be true again, but she knew that her home was beside Razor, no matter where he was.

"It won't be forever, honey," Razor assured.

"It won't be," the judge added. "You just have to be patient and trust the system. Wouldn't it be better to give the thumb drive to the proper authorities and know that you will not only be putting away Mr. Francoli but possibly the Manzoni family? You'll be free then."

"Will I be though?" Firefly asked. "What happens if the Manzoni family just puts another head of the family in place and comes after me for what I did?"

"She's right," Razor agreed. "We will need to stay hidden, but I think that we can do that in plain sight," he said.

"How?" Firefly asked.

"Well, I'm assuming that everyone up in Boston knows you as Penny Quinn," he said.

"Right," she agreed. "I never told anyone up there my MC name. I didn't want anyone to be able to find me if someone from Savage Hell came looking for me. Not many people in the club know me as Penny Quinn," she said.

"Right, so let's change your name legally to Firefly," he said.

"Firefly Quinn isn't different enough for anyone to not come sniffing around, Razor," she said.

"Right, but I'm thinking we change it to Firefly Tracy," he said. "You know, if you'd agree to marry me, we could change your last name."

"I can't marry you just to change my last name, Razor," she chided.

"No, but you can marry me because I'm head over heels in love with you, Firefly. I'm crazy about you and if you feel the same way about me, we have good reason to get hitched," he said.

The judge cleared her throat, smiling up at both of them. "I'd be happy to marry both of you," she offered. "That is, if Penny says, yes," she added. "I can also sign off on your name change too."

"Well, that would make things so much easier," Firefly said. She had fallen in love with Razor the first night she spent with him. He was easy to love and when she left, he kept a piece of her heart with him, he just didn't know it.

"I could marry you just for sake of convenience, but then, there's the who thing about me being in love with you." She smiled up at him and giggled when he blew out the breath that he must have been holding. "I'll marry you, Razor, not just to change my name, but because I'm madly in love with you too."

He picked her up and spun her around, making her squeal and the nurse ducked her head into the small room and shushed them. "I think we might have worn out our welcome," Firefly said.

"We have to meet Bowie anyway. Our time is up," Razor said.

"How about you both stop by tomorrow and I'll have everything in order. I can get my office to send over a marriage license and the paperwork for the name change," the judge offered.

"I appreciate that," Firefly said. "Could we also have Garret's name changed? I want him to have Razor's last name too. I listed him as Garret's father on the birth certificate but gave the baby my last name."

"I'd love for our son to have my last name, honey," Razor said. "Thank you."

"That would make him a junior," Firefly said. "Are you good with that?"

"I'd love that," Razor agreed. "It would be perfect."

"Well, I can't wait to meet little Garret and marry his mom and dad," the judge said. "You have my number, Penny—um, I mean, Firefly. Just text when you are ready to come over and be snuck up to my room."

"Are you sure that you're up for all of this?" Firefly asked.

"I can't think of any better medicine than to marry the two of you. Just make me one promise," the judge said. "When all of the paperwork is finished, you will turn over the thumb drive to the authorities. Turn it in down here. I'm betting that the Manzoni family's reach doesn't extend down here. In fact, I know just the person to turn it over to. He's a captain on the local force. His name is Joel Swensen."

"I know Joel," Razor said. "He was involved in a case with one of my MC brothers, Axel. He seems like a good guy. He even comes by Savage Hell once in a while to have a beer with Axel. I think he'd be perfect to turn the flash drive over to, honey," he said.

"Sounds like we have a plan," Firefly agreed. "We're getting married tomorrow then."

"I love the sound of that plan, honey," Razor agreed. "Thanks for everything, Judge."

"No problem," she agreed, settling back in her bed. "Now get out and let me get some rest." Firefly giggled and bent to kiss her cheek.

"Thank you," Firefly said. "For everything." The Judge squeezed her hand.

"My pleasure," she whispered as they turned to leave.

Razor took her hand into his own, leading her back down the hallway. "Do you really think that changing my name will keep us safe after I turn over the evidence?" she asked.

"I don't know, honey, but it's a start. Plus, I plan on building us a house in the middle of nowhere with a shit ton of security around it. You have my word, honey. I will do my very best to keep you and our son safe." She knew that Razor would too. He had always kept his promises to her, and she knew that he would do his best to keep his word to her now.

※ ※ ※

Bowie had their six while they drove back to Savage Hell. Changing their plans wasn't part of the deal, but Firefly was so happy that Razor had asked her to marry him, she didn't mind having to make new plans. Of course, they'd need Savage's help to make everything happen, but she knew that he would have their backs.

"You're here," Savage said, peeking in on Garret sleeping in his car seat. "I thought that the plan was for you to meet Ryder back at the hanger and fly back to West Virginia."

"Well, we need to come up with a new plan," Razor said.

"The judge believes that if we hand over the flash drive to Axel's friend, Joel, we could have a chance at some sort of normalcy."

"I'm listening," Savage said. "But we should continue this conversation back at our house. If you're going to stay in town, then you'll need a safe place to stay. How about you guys follow us over to the house and then, we can discuss this new plan," Savage offered.

"I don't know how we'll ever repay you for all of your help, Savage," Firefly said.

"Don't even worry about that," he said. "I promised your mom that I'd watch out for you. Paying me back isn't necessary."

"I appreciate that," she said.

Savage nodded and grabbed his truck keys from behind the bar. "You know the way, right?" he asked. Both Firefly and Razor nodded. They had both been back to Savage's home on separate occasions. "Great," he breathed, "see you both there." Savage left through the back door and Firefly took Razor's hand, he held Garrett's car seat in the other.

It didn't take them long to load the baby into the car and drive back to Savage's place. He had built his home on the same property as the bar, just a few miles back in the woods, off the beaten path.

"Something like this," Razor whispered more to himself than to her.

"Sorry," she said.

"I'm thinking that we need to build something like this.

Off the main roads, no one around. It's secluded and with the security system that I'll have installed, no one will be able to get to us unless we want them to." That sounded perfect to her, but first, they had to find a place like this to build.

"We'll have to start looking for property," she said.

"I already own the perfect land to build on. It's about twenty minutes out of town, but it's secluded and will give us enough space to build the house that we want."

"You want a big house?" she asked.

"Yeah—and a big family. You up for that, honey?" She looked back at their son in the backseat and smiled at Razor. "I think that I can handle a big family," she agreed. "Especially since this time around, I'll have help."

"Always," he agreed. "I can't wait to be a part of the whole process this time," he admitted. Hearing him say that made her feel guilty all over again and right now, they didn't have time for guilt. They needed to come up with a plan that would allow her and Razor to sneak back into the hospital to get married. Then, they'd need a place to lay low while their new place was being built. None of this seemed easy to her, but with Razor by her side, holding her hand, it felt possible.

"Ready?" she asked. She got Garret out of his car seat, and he snuggled into her body. "Poor guy," she whispered patting his back. "You've been cooped up in that thing all day, haven't you?" Garret stretched and made little noises as if agreeing with her.

"How about I change his diaper and feed him while you fill in the guys?" Razor asked.

"Me?" she squeaked. "Why am I the one who has to fill them in?"

"Because you know the judge better than I do and well, the guys will give me shit over settling down, but they won't do that with you. In fact, I'm betting Savage will want to be there to give you away tomorrow."

"That's not necessary," she said.

"Well, it kind of is," he challenged. "We will need witnesses."

"How about if we ask Savage, Dallas, and Bowie to be our witnesses?" Razor asked. Firefly quickly nodded, not able to think of anyone better than the three of them to be with her and Razor on their special day.

"Great," he said, taking the baby from her. "You fill them in and when I'm finished with Garret, I'll join you and we can ask them together."

"Sounds good," she said. Firefly looked up to find Savage standing at the front door, waiting for them.

"You two coming in or are you going to stand there clucking like hens for the rest of the day?" he teased.

"Coming," Razor grumbled. "He knows that I hate when he says shit like that," he mumbled to her. Firefly giggled and followed the two men into the farmhouse. Savage's place always felt like a warm hug—it felt like home, and she hoped that their place would feel the same when it was finished.

"I'm going to change and feed the baby," Razor said. "Can I use the nursery?"

"Absolutely," Dallas said, "you should find everything that you need in there, just don't wake up the baby."

"No promises," Razor said. "Little dude here is as noisy as his mama." Firefly slapped at his arm as he disappeared up the stairs.

"Want to fill us in?" Savage asked, nodding to the kitchen chair in front of her.

Firefly sat at the table and sighed. "Razor and I are getting married," she announced.

"Married?" Savage asked. "I thought that this was about turning over the flash drive you have to Axel's friend, Joel."

"It is," she agreed, "but, the plan starts with us getting married. I can't stay hidden away forever," she insisted. "I toyed with the idea of changing my name legally to Firefly since everyone up north knows me as Penny, but I'd still have the same last name. So, Razor came up with the plan for us to get married, and then, Garret and I can take his last name."

"That's no reason to get hitched," Savage growled. "You can change your name to whatever you want and not have to marry Razor."

"Right, but the truth is, I love him, Savage. And he says he loves me, so I think that getting married is a good next step. We want a life together and we don't want to have to hide away to do it."

"There will still be a paper trail," Bowie said. She had thought about that too. Changing her name wasn't going to be enough to stave off the Manzoni family.

"I know, and that's where we'll need your help. We want to move back, but we know we can't do that until it's safe. The judge thinks I should hand over my evidence to Axel's friend, Joel, and then, she wants me to go into witness protection until the case can play out in court. With what I have, Marcos Francoli will go to prison for a long time and probably end up taking most of the Manzoni family with him. At least, that's the plan. Then, Razor and I will be able to move back here. He has a property just out of town, and we want to build on it."

"We have some guys in the club who work in the trades," Dallas said. "Would they be able to help Razor and Firefly out?" she asked her husband.

Savage nodded, "Yep," he agreed. "I'm sure that they'd be happy to lend a hand. Anything for a brother, you all know that." He pulled Firefly into his arms and gave her one of his famous bear hugs. "You sure that you want to marry that guy?" he asked.

"Hey," Razor grumbled, walking into the room. "Watch trying to persuade my woman not to marry me. She's already said yes—no take backs," he teased, pulling her from Savage's arms into his own.

"I wouldn't ever want to take it back, Razor," she assured. She looked up at Savage who had almost become a big brother to her since her mother died. "And to answer your question, yes, I want to marry him. And—" She looked over at Razor whose sour expression made her almost want to laugh.

"Well, now I almost don't want to ask them," Razor said. "I mean, Savage did just try to get you to dump my ass."

Firefly rolled her eyes and took his hand. "We want the three of you to be with us on our big day," she said.

"Of course," Savage quickly agreed. "Wouldn't miss it—have you set a date?"

"Um, yes," she squeaked, "tomorrow."

"Wait—you two are getting married tomorrow?" Bowie asked.

"Yep," Firefly said. "The judge will marry us in her hospital room, and I can't imagine a better person to do the job. We'd love for the three of you to join us, but we understand if it's short notice and you can't."

"Tomorrow works for us," Savage insisted.

"I'll call the babysitter, and then, you and I can rummage through my closet for something for you to wear. We're about the same size," Dallas said.

"Thank you," Firefly said. Honestly, she didn't care if she had to get married in her jeans and t-shirt, but it would be nice to look pretty for her big day. "Thank you all for doing this for us."

"Not a problem," Savage said. "That's what family is for, Firefly."

RAZOR

Razor wasn't sure why he was so damn nervous, but he was. It wasn't like they were having a big wedding or standing up in front of a crowd of people. Savage's family was like his family and the judge was someone he'd known for years. All he could think about was Firefly coming to her senses and running away from him again.

He never imagined himself the marrying type, but when he asked her to be his wife, he could think of nothing that he wanted more than for her to say, yes. He was finally going to have the family that he never knew that he wanted and that made him happy and worried at the same time. Razor didn't think he deserved to be so happy, but he was going to pretend that he did because there was no way that he planned on giving Firefly or Garret back once they became his.

Razor's Edge

They got to the hospital early. In fact, the nurse chided him that they were too early for visiting hours but then, the judge pulled some strings with her doctor and had them all brought back to her room. The ceremony was perfect, even with Garret fussing the entire time, he couldn't have planned a better day. And when the judge told him to kiss his bride, he didn't hesitate to pull Firefly against his body and kiss her like he had never kissed anyone before. She was his wife, the mother of his son, and now, his whole future.

After the marriage license and name change paperwork was signed—all the t's crossed and I's dotted, they said their goodbyes and snuck back out of the hospital. It was almost as if nothing had happened up in the judge's hospital room—that his life hadn't just completely changed and given him two amazing gifts.

Neither of them spoke a word to the other until they were about ten minutes away from the hospital. They had strapped Garret's car seat in and jumped into the SUV to make a quick getaway, just as they had planned the day before at Savage's place. They knew that they were taking a chance by going in to see the judge, but he didn't care. He walked out of there with his new wife and son, and that was all he could think about—not the danger that possibly lurked around every corner.

"I can't believe we just did that," Firefly whispered, breaking the silence that had trailed them for the last ten miles. "Did that really just happen?" she asked.

"Yes," he breathed, reaching across the console to take her

hand into his own. "You having regrets already?" he teased. He worried that he had just guessed correctly, but he didn't want to let on what he was thinking.

"No," she breathed. "No regrets. Are you having regrets?" she asked.

He squeezed her hand into his. "Never," he assured. "Marrying you was the best decision that I ever made," he said. "Well, that and asking you to have a drink with me after your court date."

"Um, I believe that I was the one who asked you to have a drink with me, after my court date," she corrected. He knew she was right, but he liked giving her shit.

"You sure about that, honey?" he teased.

"Yes," she spat. "I found you lurking in the hallway after my meeting with the judge and that's when I asked you to have a beer with me, to thank you for coming down to the courthouse to help me."

"I don't lurk," he insisted.

"Whatever, but I was the one who asked you to go to Savage Hell, at least admit that much to be true," she said.

"I'm guessing that with both of us being lawyers, this is how most of our married spats will go?" he asked. He loved that she could give as good as he could. She was always keep him on his toes and that was something he'd never tire of. He married his perfect match.

"This is not a spat," she insisted. "It's a disagreement."

"Same thing," he countered. "I think that after we have

newlywed sex, we should jump right into make-up sex. I hear it's all the rage," he teased.

He pulled her hand up to his lips. "You okay?" he asked.

"I'm just worried about the next few months," she admitted. "I hate that we have to fly back to Savage's cabin in West Virginia. I wish we could just stay home, but I also know it's not safe."

"I know," he said. They had left the thumb drive with Savage. He promised to head right over to the station and turn it over to Joel, but he still had his concerns. Savage had a good point—taking Firefly and Garret down to the police station wasn't a good idea, since she might be spotted. Savage would be able to slip in and out of the station, without drawing much attention to himself. If the Manzoni family was watching, they wouldn't know who the big guy was or what he was doing downtown. The rest of the plan involved them meeting Ryder at the hanger and flying back to West Virginia while the judge worked her magic and pulled a few strings.

"I promise that I'll take you someplace nice for a honeymoon as soon as this thing is over," he assured. "I know that you probably didn't imagine having to get married in a hospital room or spending our first few months as husband and wife in a run-down cabin," he said. "I promise to make this all up to you."

"You have nothing to make up to me, Razor," she insisted. "I loved our ceremony. All the people who matter most to me were in that room. As for being locked away with you and

Garret in Savage's cabin, it's not so bad. I mean, I do get you all to myself while we wait the trial out. I think we should take advantage of our alone time and maybe work on expanding our family."

"Another baby?" he asked. "You want to have another one?"

"Yes," she said. "I want to share everything we didn't get to share the first time around. I'm the one who has some making up to do to you, Razor. Let me start making up for walking away from you the first time."

"I told you that you have nothing to make up for that, honey," he said. "But I'd love to try for another baby. I think the first one that we made is pretty damn cute."

"He is," she agreed, looking into the back seat. "I guess you're going to have to add a few extra bedrooms to the house plans," she said.

"I'm all for it, honey," he agreed. "We can come up with a plan and then, I'll have the guys get started on building your dream home."

"I feel like the luckiest girl in the world," she whispered. "I never imagined that asking you our for a beer would land us here," she said.

"Well, asking you back to my place helped. I mean, we did make Garret that night. If I hadn't seduced you with my charm and good looks, you wouldn't be my wife now," he teased.

Her giggle filled the cabin of the car and it sounded magical. "Yeah, that's how you seduced me—with your charm and good looks. And despite all of that, I still agreed to be your wife. You are one lucky man, Razor," she teased. She was right about one thing—he was lucky to have found her. He had found the woman of his dreams sitting behind the defendant's table in that courtroom. He'd fallen for her sassy, kickass, capable attitude and now, she was his wife. That truly made him the luckiest bastard on the planet.

The End

I hope you enjoyed Razor and Firefly's story. Now, buckle up for your inside sneak peek at Trista's Truth (Savage Hell Book 7).

JOEL

JOEL WALKED INTO THE BAR TO FIND AXEL AND MELODY sitting up at the bar, the last thing he wanted was a night out, but he had promised his former partner and her new husband that he'd meet them for a beer to celebrate them getting hitched. Actually, they had been married for almost six months now, and he had been promising to meet them at Savage Hell, for weeks on end, but he was always too tired after his shift to join them for a few beers. He planned on canceling on them again tonight but then, he ran into Melody, and she threatened to hunt him down and drag his ass into the bar for a night out. He protested, saying that he was tired and just wanted to collapse into bed, but she reminded him that tomorrow was Saturday and he'd be able to sleep in. She took away any argument that he had and not showing up wasn't an option.

As soon as Axel and Melody saw him, they smiled and waved in unison, and he could feel his eyes roll. He found what everyone else thought of as adorable, to be annoying, although he kept that to himself. He'd never want them to think that he was jealous about the two of them being together. Melody was not just his partner on the force, she was also his ex-girlfriend. She was the one who had gotten away, and he might be over losing her, he still didn't find her and her new husband to be cute, adorable, or a perfect couple as others had called them.

"Good to see that you could make it," Melody said.

"Well, I didn't like the alternatives presented to me earlier today, if I didn't show up," he grumbled.

"Tell me you didn't threaten the guy, honey," Axel said.

"She came into my office today to let me know that turning down your invitation again would end up with a manhunt—involving yours truly and your new, blushing bride."

Axel chuckled, seeming to miss the point of Melody telling her new boss that she'd hunt him down and drag his ass to the bar, to be completely inappropriate. "I think your idea of funny and my idea of funny are very different," Joel grumbled. He waved down the bartender and asked for another round of beers and sat up on the barstool next to Axel.

"Well, getting you here tonight was kind of important to us," she said.

"Why's that?" Joel asked.

"We have someone that we want you to meet," Melody said.

"No," Joel simply said. "No setups. I thought that we've been through all of this before. I don't want to date right now. I just don't have time for it since my promotion. You know how many hours I put in at the station. I don't have time for any extracurriculars," Joel insisted.

"I know how hard you work, Joel," Melody said. "It's why I want to introduce you to my friend, Trista. She's perfect for you and you can't be serious about not dating. Work can't be your entire life. You need to find a work/personal life balance, or you'll wake up one day, all alone, and it will be too late."

"I have some time before that happens, Melody," he assured.

"You're turning forty this year, Joel. You need to diversify, branch out and maybe, just maybe you'll realize that work isn't everything," Melody insisted.

"Just give Trista a chance," Axel chimed in. He knew that he wasn't going to get the final word in all of this. Once Melody set her mind to something, she'd find a way to make it happen. And with Axel taking her side, she'd be relentless.

"Fine," Joel mumbled. "I'll meet this friend of yours, but I'm making no promises," he said.

"At least have a beer with her," Axel said. "Talk to her, maybe even get to know the woman a little bit. She might surprise you, man." He hated surprises, and he had half a mind to tell Axel that, but it was too late. They had roped him into the bar only to ambush him with a fix-up. This whole evening was turning into one giant surprise, and he hated everything about it.

"I know that this is way out of your comfort zone, Joel," Melody said. "But I worry about you. We were close once, and just because that didn't work out doesn't mean that I don't still worry about you."

"While I appreciate that, Melody," he said. "I hate surprises—you know that. Remember how I reacted to that surprise birthday party you threw me at the precinct?"

"Oh, I remember that birthday," Melody said. "You shouted at me for about ten minutes and then stormed out of the break room. You were a jerk, but we ate your cake anyway, and eventually, you got over it."

"I've never gotten over it if we're being honest here. I hate surprises, and now, you're having me meet a complete stranger at a bar and you think it's a good thing?" he asked.

"Just don't throw a fit and stomp out of here," Melody said.

"No promises," he said.

Melody popped up from her barstool and squealed, clapping her hands. "She's here," she gushed.

"As if we couldn't tell," Axel teased. She ran across the bar and hugged her friend. "Trista's not bad looking, right?"

He turned around to look her over, knowing full well that he was going to find her wanting no matter what she looked like. He was being an ass and that had everything to do with how tired he was. "She's not bad," Joel admitted. She was more than not bad but admitting that out loud would be equivalent to admitting that Melody might be right and that was a dangerous game to play. She loved to make him tell her that she was right, at any cost, and he usually tried like hell to avoid having to do it.

Melody and Trista walked across the barroom and just about every guy in the place watched them make their way over to the bar. Trista was a beautiful woman, but that didn't make any of this setup feel right to him.

"Joel," Melody said, her arm around her friend, "this is Trista Stonewell. Trista, this is Joel Swensen."

"It's good to meet you," Trista said, holding out her hand to him. He took her hand into his own, noting the way his skin felt a bit tingly just by her touch.

"Good to meet you too, Trista," Joel said. He sat there like an idiot, holding onto her hand, not realizing that he hadn't let go of it until she pulled it free from his.

"Can I buy you a beer?" he asked.

Trista shook her head and reached into her purse, pulling out a gun and pointing it at his chest. "No, thank you," she said.

"What the hell?" Melody shouted. "What are you doing?"

"What I have to do," Trista whispered. "I'm sorry Melody."

TRISTA

Trista wasn't sure how this was supposed to go. Her instructions were clear—find Joel Swensen and bring him in alive, by any means necessary. Keeping her job a secret from her friend while she got close to Joel's ex-partner wasn't easy. Working for the CIA was something that she loved but lying for a living wasn't something that she enjoyed doing. She looked at it as part of the job—lying to her friends and family had become a part of her life, even if she hated doing it.

"You will need to come with me Mr. Swensen," Trista ordered.

"And why would I do that?" Joel asked. His slight smirk told her that he thought he had the upper hand in all of this, but he was wrong. He might be a good cop, but she was better. It's why she eventually was recruited to join the CIA.

"For your own safety," she insisted.

Joel barked out his laugh, "It seems to me that the only person threatening my safety is you, honey," he said.

"How about you put the gun down and tell us what this is all about, Trista?" Axel asked.

"Can't," Trista said. If she involved Axel and Melody in this, they wouldn't be safe. She needed to get Joel out of there and then, hope that nobody was following her. It was going to be her best option to keep him safe. The men that he had looking for him were bad news and if she involved her friends, they'd be next on their list of targets.

"It wouldn't be safe for either of you to get involved in this," she breathed. She pulled her badge out of her jacket pocket and quickly flashed it at them. "I'm CIA and you're in trouble, Joel."

"So, it's Joel now?" he asked. "What happened to Mr. Swensen?"

"If I'm going to help you, we should be on a first name basis. The men who are after you won't care what I call you, really," she said.

"Men who are after me?" he questioned. "And who might they be?"

"The Gemini Brothers," she leaned in to whisper. "I believe that you took down their gang's leader a few months ago, and they're looking for retribution."

"Why would any of this be on the CIA's radar?" Joel asked.

"Because we had a man on the inside when you took

down the lead suspect. We need your help releasing Dante Gemini so that we can bring down their entire operation. It's the only way to stop them and their human trafficking ring."

"Wait, you said that the Gemini Brothers were after me, but this is about letting a known murderer go?" he asked. "Why would I do that?"

"Because the Gemini Brothers are after the same thing. They want Dante released from prison, but they won't stop there. They'll kill anyone close to you to get you to comply, and when you do, they'll murder you too. If you agree to work with me and the CIA, we'll get him released, but no one will have to end up dead."

"Except the countless people who get in Dante's way. What happens when he's free and goes on a revenge killing spree?" Joel asked. "Because you and I both know that's what will happen, Trista."

She shrugged, "We just have to be one step ahead of him and keep anyone else from getting killed. The CIA needs time to be able to bring him and his family down. We want all of the big players, not just the head of the family. Dante being in prison doesn't make him less powerful. They just put another head in place and Dante controls the family from prison. You have to be smart enough to understand that, Joel. I mean, you seem like a bright guy."

"Gee, thanks for that," Joel grumbled.

"You know what I mean, Joel. I didn't intend to insult you in any way. I need for you to come with me—you're not safe here. And everyone around you is in danger. Do you want that for Melody and Axel?" Trista asked.

"Oh—so now you care about me and my husband?" Melody questioned. "You used me to get to Joel. I thought that you were my friend, Trista," she spat.

"I was your friend," she breathed. "I'd still like to be, but the unfortunate part of my job is that sometimes, I have to lie to my friends."

"By lie, you mean you have to make up an entirely different life to feed to me, right? You told me that you're a nurse," she said. "That's what you do for a living, right? You lie."

"Well, it wasn't totally a lie. I was a nurse at one point—in the military. I served my time, and when I got out, I decided that I didn't want to become a private practice nurse, so I went into the police academy instead. I was good at being a cop, and that's when the CIA took notice of me and hired me to be an agent. There, now you know everything that there is to know about me," Trista promised.

Melody stuck her nose up in the air and made a little humming noise. "I'm sure that isn't the case. I'm betting that you have a few more secrets that you aren't sharing with us." She had a lot more secrets, too many to tell, and that's the way she'd keep it too.

She looked back over at Joel as if effectively dismissing Melody and her comments. "So, what's it going to be, Joel?" she asked. She was still holding her gun at him, pointing it at his chest, but she thought that she'd at least let him believe that he had a choice in the matter. The truth of it was that she wasn't going to leave the bar without Joel by her side. Those were her orders and she always followed orders to the letter.

"You going to stay here and possibly get all of these people killed or are you going to come with me and help out the CIA?" she asked.

"Do I really have a choice in the matter?" he grumbled. She wanted to tell him that he didn't, but that would just be like rubbing salt in his wounds. Joel didn't seem like the type of man who took orders from others well. In fact, she was sure of it with the way that he had worked his way up the ranks to Captain so quickly.

"If I told you yes, you wouldn't believe me," she said.

"Probably because it would be another lie," Joel hissed. "Fine, let's get this shit show over with. I'll tell your superiors what I've already told you. I can't just release Dante Gemini. I'm not the person to give that order. You think that I have more power than I actually do, Trista."

She laughed, "You and I both know that's just not true, Joel. You have all the power here," she assured.

"Yet, you're the one pointing a gun at me," he accused. He stood and nodded to Melody and Axel. "Thanks for a great night out, guys," he drawled. "And thanks so much for introducing me to Trista, it's been a blast." She nodded for him to walk in front of her, so that she could keep her gun pointed at his back.

"Let's go, Joel," she said. "We have a long drive ahead of

us." She didn't bother to look back at either Melody or Axel. She knew that she had burned her bridges with her new friends and there would be no point. All she needed to focus on now was getting Joel back to headquarters in one peace and knowing the Gemini Brothers, that was going to take a freaking miracle.

Trista's Truth (Savage Hell Book 7) coming November 2022!!
Don't miss the other books in the Savage Hell series! These titles are available NOW!

RoadKill-> https://books2read.com/u/bWPeRM
REPOssession->https://books2read.com/u/bMXDa5
Dirty Ryder->https://books2read.com/u/3RnyxR
Hart's Desire-> https://books2read.com/u/bpzJ9k
Axel's Grind-> https://books2read.com/u/3Gw9oK
Razor's Edge-> https://books2read.com/u/m0lepY

Also, don't miss K.L.'s Royal Bastards! The Royal Bastards are the series that started it all and led to the spinoff of Savage Hell!!! Savage Heat (RBMC Book 1) is available NOW!! Here's an inside look at the book that started it all!

SAVAGE

SAVAGE WATCHED AS HIS LATEST FAILURE FLOATED DOWN FROM the atmosphere back to earth. At least this time the damn parachute deployed, and he wouldn't have to start from scratch again to rebuild his rocket. Last time that happened, his boss threw a major fit, telling him to get his shit and clear out of his office. A short week later, his boss was standing on Savage's front porch, proverbial hat in hand, begging him to come back to work. He even gave him some bullshit about the government needing his service and all that shit. Savage didn't have the desire to tell his boss that he had not only served his government for almost twenty years, but he had also had the bullet holes and shrapnel in his leg to prove it.

Sure, he could sit around and complain about his past and waking up every day in pain, but where would that get him. It was his choice to join the Air Force and it was his choice to re-up when he could have gotten out. He saw active combat for the third time and that was when his copter went down and most of his buddies died. There was nothing he could have done differently that day but God, it was just about all he could think about every night when he laid down and tried to sleep. Their faces would flicker through his memories, and he knew that he was going to have another restless night ahead. It was who he had become since he was honorably discharged.

Of course, the Army was quick to jump on his specific skill set and make him the best fucking job offer he'd ever gotten. How could he refuse and why would he? He got to stay in Huntsville, Alabama, where his kid could stay in the same school with the only friends she had ever known. Uprooting Chloe wasn't part of his plan—the poor kid hadn't had much stability in her life. Chloe wasn't really his kid, but that wasn't something he liked to think about too often. It brought up too many bad memories and he tried to only look forward, never back.

Savage adopted Chloe when she was just six months old after her mother and father died in a horrible auto accident. She was his niece and when child services showed up at his doorstep with a baby in tow, claiming that his estranged sister had given him full custody in her will, what was he supposed to do? Savage didn't have one fucking idea how to take care of a kid and they were handing him one that still needed twenty-four-seven care. He quickly learned how to change a diaper and what to feed and not feed a six-month-old. Honestly, that last part was learned the hard way because the kid ended up not being able to handle table food at such an early age. Everything he fed her seemed to run through her like sand in a sieve. But that was all behind him now. He wasn't sure how he would have survived without that little girl. She had become his whole reason for living. Hell, she basically saved his life and gave him purpose and the will to keep going after his accident.

He had only been home for a few months when Chloe came into his life, and he was feeling pretty down and sorry for himself. Both of his parents were gone. His father was never really in the picture and his mom died the year he graduated from high school. Her death had sent him into a spiral that led to him joining the Air Force after he graduated. It also was one of the reasons his older sister, Cherry, stopped talking to him. She begged him not to go into the military; even tried to guilt him into feeling bad about leaving her with no one, since both of their parents were gone. But he didn't listen. Hell, the only thing Savage wanted to do was ride his damn motorcycle and get the fuck out of that town. He was a punk-ass kid who didn't know any better and the day he left to enlist was the last time he saw Cherry alive.

Now, every time he looked at Chloe's sweet face, he saw his sister. He never met Chloe's dad, but he had heard that his sister met a good guy and got married. He liked to imagine Cherry happy with her beautiful new family, at least for a little while. She deserved some happiness after all the shit life had thrown at her, including a punk-ass, eighteen-year-old kid brother who thought he knew better than she did. God was he wrong. His relationship with Cherry was the one thing he regretted in life, but Savage learned that regrets would only hold him back and he couldn't allow that. He had too much going for him to wallow in self-pity.

"I think your rocket's a dud." Savage turned to find the hot guy who always seemed to follow him around Redstone Arsenal. It was as if the guy was his personal bodyguard with the way he watched Savage and he had to admit, he wouldn't mind having his body guarded by him.

"Yeah, well, this is literally rocket science, so I can't really use that old line." Savage looked the guy up and down, liking the way he filled out his fatigues. Not having to wear a uniform was one of the many perks of no longer being enlisted. He usually wore ratty old jeans and a t-shirt when he was on base, partially out of defiance but mostly for comfort. The Alabama heat was quite unbearable, but he was used to it. He never really lived anywhere else with the exception of being stationed overseas.

"I'm Bowie Wolfe," the guy said, holding out his hand, waiting for Savage to take it.

He shook the younger guy's hand and smiled. "Are you named after the singer?" Savage questioned.

"Yeah," he breathed. "My mother was a huge fan and well, I got stuck with the name."

Savage shrugged, "All in all, I'd say you did all right. David Bowie is a legend, man," he said.

Bowie groaned and laughed. "Yeah, now you just sound like my mother," he teased.

"Thanks for that," Savage grumbled. He knew just by looking at the guy that he had a few years on him. Hell, he had more than a few years but that usually didn't bother him. Savage liked his guys young and feisty.

"Sorry, man. Um, I didn't catch your name," Bowie said.

"Savage," he offered.

"Wow—you gave me shit about my name but yours is pretty epic too. How did you get a name like Savage?" Bowie crossed his arms over his massive chest and waited him out. It wasn't something Savage liked to talk about, but the determination on the guy's face told him he really had no choice in the matter.

"Savage is actually my last name. My first name is Logan, but my club gave me the nickname after I told them about my helicopter going down. Lost a lot of good guys that day and my buddies said I'm still alive because I'm too savage to die."

"You served?" Bowie asked.

"Yeah—career Air Force until the accident and then honorably discharged," Savage admitted. "How about you?" Bowie held his arms wide as if showing Savage his fatigues to prove his point.

"I enlisted in the Army right from high school and haven't left yet. I've been in for twelve years now and I hope to make this my career, but we'll see." Savage did the math in his head and whistled.

"So, you're what—about thirty?" he questioned.

"I'll be thirty-one in a few months," Bowie admitted.

"You're just a kid," Savage teased.

"Yeah—okay, old man," Bowie said. Savage knew the guy was teasing but at forty-five, he was really beginning to feel his age. "And how old are you?" Savage winced at the mention of his age. It was something he usually didn't share because it wasn't anyone's damn business.

Savage smiled at Bowie, trying to deflect his question with one of his own. "Want to have a couple of beers with me?" Savage knew he was pushing his luck with the younger guy, but he didn't give a shit. He was hot, tired and Bowie turned him the fuck on. It was time to knock off and if Savage could convince him to have a couple of beers, then he might be able to talk Bowie into coming home with him for the night. If he was reading the signals correctly, his new friend was interested but he had been wrong in the past—so who knew.

"You asking me out, Savage?" Bowie questioned. Now it was Savage's turn to waiver in his answer and he suddenly worried that he had misread the chemistry that hummed through the air between the two of them.

Savage shrugged, "Maybe I am," he said, not really answering Bowie's question. The guy was as stoic as they came and Savage was trying to read him, but he wasn't having any luck.

"Listen, if I misread the situation, then just forget I asked," Savage grumbled. He picked up the last part of his rocket that landed a few hundred feet away from where he had parked and by the time he turned around and headed back to his pick-up truck, he found Bowie leaning up against the passenger side door, his hands shoved deep into his pockets.

"I'm in," Bowie said, flashing him a wolfish grin.

"Sounds good," Savage said. He was trying for nonchalant, but his tone sounded anything but. It had been a damn long time since he met a man who made his cock pay attention, but Bowie did that for him. Savage needed to get himself under control or he'd blow his whole cool guy routine. Hell, he was far from being cool, but Bowie seemed interested, and he wasn't about to do anything to fuck that up.

"You have someplace in mind?" Bowie asked, helping Savage shove the last of his equipment into the back of his pickup. "I mean, do you have a place you usually go to, you know, for a few beers?"

Savage liked the way Bowie seemed just as flustered about their situation as he was. He found it kind of cute the way the guy was floundering for words. He could have helped him out but giving him a hard time felt like the better option and would be a lot more fun.

"You mean, like a gay bar?" Savage asked. He knew he was adding fuel to the fire, but he didn't care. Bowie turned an adorable shade of red that ran down his sexy neck and had Savage wanting to see just how far down his blush went.

"Well, I mean—sure. Or any bar, for that matter. It doesn't matter to me," Bowie stuttered.

Savage reached out and put his hand on Bowie's arm. "I'm just messing with you," he said. "I don't know of too many gay bars in Huntsville. I usually just go to my own bar, but I don't really advertise that I'm gay and I don't feel like answering questions tonight. You mind just going to the Voodoo Lounge? It's a bit yuppie but I think we can blend in with the regular crowd. Plus, they've got great live music a few nights of the week."

"Wait—you have a bar?" Bowie asked.

Savage smiled and nodded, "Yep—the bar's called Savage Hell. It's also where my motorcycle club meets. We're a part of the Royal Bastards, which is a nationwide MC, but my little chapter calls themselves Savage Hell, after the bar. I try to keep my personal and private lives separate."

"Meaning you haven't shared that you're gay with your club," Bowie guessed.

Savage wasn't sure what to say to Bowie's assessment. On the one hand, he felt the need to set him straight and on the other, he wanted to tell him it wasn't anyone's business who he was having sex with. From the way his body was responding to Bowie, he hoped to have sex with him before the end of the night.

"Listen," Savage said. "I learned a long time ago that who I'm fucking is no one's business. I like you, Bowie but if you're not interested, tell me now if I'm wasting my time."

"I was just talking, man," Bowie said.

Savage sighed, "Yeah—I'm just on edge lately with these damn tests needing to be done yesterday and I'm being an ass. Sorry," he offered. "And to answer your question—I haven't told my club that I'm bi." Hell, he hadn't told many people about that part of his life. Savage was careful not to bring any of the men or women he slept with home to meet Chloe. He didn't want to expose his daughter to his unstable dating life and that was exactly what it was —chaotic.

He hadn't been much of a serial dater, usually not making it past one night with a person. It was easier that way. He didn't have to make any promises to anyone, and he didn't expect anything in return. The one time he broke his no dating rule, he ended up running away like a fucking coward when messy feelings got in the way.

"So, we doing this?" Savage asked. He started for the driver's side of his pick-up, not waiting to see if Bowie was going to join him or not.

"I get it," Bowie said. "I don't share that part of my life easily. I haven't even come out to my family yet." Bowie slipped into the passenger side of the cab of the truck and pulled his seatbelt on, clicking it in place.

"What about your truck?" Savage asked, nodding to where Bowie's vehicle sat, just down the road.

"I'll get it tomorrow when I'm back on duty. That is if you don't mind giving me a lift back to my place later." Bowie seemed to assume Savage would just agree and honestly, he didn't mind. If he was Bowie's ride for the night, there was a better chance they'd end up in Bowie's bed for a little while. Savage never left Chloe overnight, but he had a sitter with her, and he knew that she'd agree to a few extra hours if he paid double.

"Sure," Savage said. "No problem."

"Thanks," Bowie said. "I have to admit, I could use a night out. It's been a shit show around base, and I could use the break."

"Yeah, I heard about the cut-backs, and I guess being down so many people makes for more work for the ones who are left." Savage knew some other guys on base from his club and they were all complaining about the changes to the budget and having to take on more hours for the same pay. His MC was made up of mostly military guys, both active and retired. But his guys came from all walks of life—he even had a few one-percenters who he was happy to help get their lives straightened out. He liked helping his guys and even took a few of them under his wing, as a sort of personal project.

"Yep, it sucks. But what am I gonna do? Uncle Sam owns me, and I go where he tells me," Bowie said.

"Where are you originally from?" Savage asked. He usually didn't get too chatty with his "dates" but there was something about Bowie that made him want to know more about the guy.

"Texas," Bowie said.

"You get homesick?" Savage questioned.

"Naw," Bowie admitted. "Like I said, I still haven't come out to my family, and keeping a secret like that weighs on a person. It's easier being away from home and not having to worry about watching my back or saying the wrong thing."

"I get that," Savage said. "I haven't exactly been forthcoming about my sexuality with my friends or family either." He had a few close buddies in his club that knew the truth and he trusted them not only with his secret but with his life.

"I'd like to blame my military background for all the secrecy, but that really isn't an issue anymore," Bowie said.

"Yeah, that wasn't the case when I enlisted." Savage had served under the "Don't ask, don't tell," era and he had to admit, it had its pros and cons. Not having people diving too deep into his personal life was always a plus. He valued his privacy over everything else.

"You originally from Huntsville?" Bowie asked.

"Yeah," Savage said. "My family was from here, but they're all gone now. Well, everyone except Chloe and me." Savage mentally kicked himself for talking about his daughter. It wasn't something he did with complete strangers, and he was starting to worry that asking Bowie out might have been a bad choice. Sure, the guy was the sexiest man he had seen in a damn long time, but he was completely blowing his rules out the fucking window with Bowie and that usually didn't end well for him.

"Who's Chloe?" Bowie asked as if he was able to read Savage's mind.

"My kid," Savage admitted.

"You have a daughter?" Bowie asked.

"She's six and I adopted her when she was a baby. Chloe is my sister's kid and when she and her husband died in a car accident, I took Chloe in."

"Wow," Bowie breathed. "I'm sorry about your sister and brother-in-law. But Chloe is lucky to have you, man."

Savage shrugged, "Thanks. And I'm the lucky one. She came into my life when I was in a dark place, and she gave me a purpose. She's a great kid."

"That makes sense," Bowie said. "She seems to have a pretty awesome dad."

BOWIE

Bowie wasn't sure how the hell he had ended up in the sexy stranger's pick-up agreeing to go for a few beers with him. He had been watching Savage for weeks now, not that he'd ever admit to it. Bowie had always been attracted to older men and Savage was his type, right down to his salt and pepper beard that made him want to give it a tug.

It had been a damn long time since he found anyone interesting enough to go out for a few beers with. When Savage first asked him out, he wasn't sure he had heard him correctly. He usually had a pretty good idea when a guy or woman, for that matter, was interested in him. But Savage didn't give him anything to go by. It was hard to get a read on the guy and that made Bowie want him even more. He always did like a challenge.

Honestly, dating men was kind of new to him. He wasn't

lying when he told Savage that he hadn't come out to his family yet. It was one of the reasons why he jumped at the chance to be transferred to Huntsville from Texas when the opportunity arose. He hated that he was taking the coward's way out, but that was easier than admitting that he was bi. He was even beginning to avoid his weekly calls home to his parents because he got sick of dodging their questions about if he had someone special in his life. Even if he had, he wouldn't be able to admit it because that would mean telling his parents who he was.

"You're awfully quiet," Savage said. "You having second thoughts?"

"About beer—never," Bowie teased. Savage shot him a smirk that told him he wasn't buying him using humor to hide from the question.

"You always a smart ass?" Savage asked.

"Most of the time," Bowie admitted. "I use humor to mask what I'm really feeling. My therapist says it's a way for me to hide my true self because I'm afraid that if people get to really know me, they won't like who I am." Bowie looked at Savage and almost made it through without busting up laughing. Savage looked about ready to pull to the side of the road and kick Bowie's ass out of his pick-up.

"Really, man," Savage grumbled. "I'm not sure if you're kidding or not." He shook his head at Bowie and smiled.

"Your face, man," Bowie said between fits of laughter.

"Yeah, yeah. Laugh it up," Savage griped. "Was any of that true?" The sad fact was it was all true, but Bowie wouldn't admit that to Savage on what could potentially be their first date.

"Naw," Bowie lied. "I just like yanking people's chains." Savage looked at him as if he was trying to decide if he wanted to believe him or not. He seemed like a smart guy and if he was telling the truth earlier, a literal rocket scientist. Bowie worried that Savage would be able to see right through his facade and that scared the hell out of him.

"I mean, I've been to a therapist, but that was to work a few things out after I got back from active duty," Bowie admitted. Giving the guy some truth might throw him off the scent. It would be best to get through the night together without Savage finding out just how messed up he really was. That was another one of his secrets he didn't share with anyone—well, besides his therapist.

"Yeah—happens to the best of us. The Air Force shoved my ass into therapy after I got shot down, not that it helped much." Bowie knew just how a tragedy like that could affect a guy. He watched his best friend die after their Humvee was attacked. It should have been him who was lying on the side of the road, bleeding out but instead, it was his best friend, Drew.

They pulled into one of Huntsville's dive bars famous for its customers being a little on the shady side. It was a perfect spot for two guys who didn't want to be seen out together, to grab a few beers. No one got into anyone else's business in places like the Voodoo Lounge and that was just the way they both seemed to want it. He knew that score—Savage didn't look like the type of guy who did long-term relationships and that was fine with Bowie. He wasn't sure where he'd be tomorrow and settling down with someone like Savage seemed like a pipe dream. He never let himself imagine his life with a man. Hell, he never imagined settling down with anyone, if he was being completely honest.

Savage parked his truck and cut the engine. "Listen, man," he sighed, "if you changed your mind about all of this, I'd get it."

Bowie smiled at Savage and reached across the center console to take his hand. "You keep saying that, Savage. But I haven't changed my mind—about the beer or you. I'd like to hang out with you tonight, no pressure and no strings. You up for that?" Savage nodded and if Bowie wasn't mistaken, he could have sworn the big guy was blushing.

"I'd like that," he said. Savage grabbed his baseball cap from the back seat and covered his bald head, running his hand down his beard and Bowie couldn't seem to take his eyes off the guy. He was hot as fuck and Bowie was mesmerized by his every movement. He had been for weeks, following him around, watching him on base. Savage was big but carried himself with confidence and grace. He had a persona that screamed alpha and that alone turned Bowie completely the fuck on. He liked older men because the few he had been with usually insisted on being in charge in the bedroom. He wondered if Savage would be just as demanding, and the thought sent a shiver down his body.

"You good?" Savage asked. Bowie shook his head and smiled.

"No, but it's nothing a few beers won't fix," Bowie lied. He had a feeling it would take more than alcohol to right what had been bothering him. In fact, Bowie had a sneaky feeling it would take at least a night of taking orders from the sexy man sitting next to him to start feeling like himself again.

SAVAGE

SAVAGE FELT ABOUT READY TO TURN BACK AROUND AND LEAVE just as soon as he saw his ex sitting at the bar with her girlfriends. Apparently, one of them was about to get hitched and Dallas was there to help her celebrate. At least, that was what he had gathered from the group of rowdy women.

"Shit," he grumbled and sat down next to Bowie. He looked down at the end of the bar to where Dallas mean-mugged him and had the nerve to laugh.

"I'd say 'shit' doesn't even begin to cover it judging from the way that blonde is scowling at you, man. What did you do?" Bowie asked. That really was a loaded question. It was more like what he didn't do that was the problem. She was the only woman that Savage dated more than just a few times. Hell, she was the only person he had any kind of relationship within his entire adult life. And he fucked it completely up with her. He ghosted Dallas when he realized he wasn't going to be able to commit to her. She'd never be enough for him and how did he admit something like that to her? It was easier to just walk away from her and hope that Dallas would just forget about him. Her angry scowl told him that hadn't happened yet.

"We dated," Savage admitted. "About a year ago."

"Wow," Bowie whistled under his breath. "So, whatever you did to that woman must have been big, if she hasn't forgiven you in a year."

"I didn't ask for forgiveness," Savage growled. "And I'm not looking for it now."

"Well, I didn't have you pegged as the dating type," Bowie said. Savage held up two fingers to the bartender, signaling that he wanted a couple of beers. The bar really didn't offer much in the way of choices and he was one of the regulars, on nights after he had a rough day at work and didn't want to deal with his MC brothers asking him a million questions. At the Voodoo Lounge, he could just be himself and no one really bothered him.

The bartender brought them their beers and a bowl of pretzels that looked like they had been set out for a few weeks. "Hey, Savage," the bartender said.

"Mike." Savage nodded. "Start me a tab," he ordered.

"Sure thing," Mike agreed and nodded to Bowie.

"You new here?" he asked.

"Yeah," Bowie said. "New to the area, really. I'm at Redstone Arsenal." Mike grunted and Bowie smiled.

"Well, women around these parts seem to burst into flames around guys in uniform. Just watch yourself with the piranhas at the end of the bar. One of the chicks is getting married but they seem to be out for a good time. Just fair warning; unless you're looking for something like that." Mike looked between Bowie and Savage as if trying to access what was going on between the two of them and Savage growled.

"Thanks, Mike," he barked, all but dismissing the guy. Bowie laughed again and he wondered what was so funny, but he had a feeling he wouldn't like Bowie's answer. So, he didn't bother asking.

"Are you always so grumbly?" Bowie accused.

"No," Savage quickly defended, shooting him a look that probably told him he was lying. Bowie held up his hands as if in defense.

"Okay, man," he said. "No need to bite my head off. If you want to go someplace else, we can. Hell, we can go back to my apartment. I have beer there." Bowie shot him a wolfish grin, making Savage smile.

"I'm good here," Savage lied. He could feel Dallas' eyes boring into the back of his head and he wasn't sure what the hell to do about her.

"Liar," Bowie challenged. "That sexy blonde has you squirming in your seat. It's hot, really—the thought of you with her. I just don't want to cause any trouble. Does she know?"

"Know what?" Savage asked, playing dumb.

Bowie sighed. "Does she know that you date guys?" he whispered.

"No," Savage breathed. He sucked down half his beer and shot a look across the bar to where Dallas was still giving him the stink-eye.

"You ghost her or something?" Bowie teased and Savaged winced. "Fuck, man," Bowie spat. "You didn't fucking ghost that hot woman sitting at the end of the bar?"

"I did and can you keep it down, man?" Savage said.

"I'm pretty sure she can't hear me over this God-awful honky-tonk music and the ruckus her girlfriends are making. Why did you do it?" Bowie asked.

"Because she would never be enough for me," Savage admitted. It was the truest thing he had said to Bowie, and he worried that made him sound like an ass. "We had been on a few dates, and I really liked her, but then I realized that if I dated her—you know, just her—I'd be denying half of myself. You know what I mean?"

Bowie nodded like he understood exactly what Savage was talking about and he realized that he had just assumed the guy was gay.

"You like women too?" Savage asked.

"Yep," Bowie admitted." In fact, I haven't been with many men. It was easier to deny that part of who I was while I was living so close to home. I didn't start exploring that side of my sexuality until I was stationed here. I had been on a few dates with men, but not a lot. So, I do get what you're talking about, man."

Savage sat back on his barstool and waved the bartender back over. "We'll take two more and buy the ladies at the end of the bar another round on me," he said. Mike nodded and walked back down to where the loud group of women sat and when he announced that Savage wanted to buy them a round of drinks, they all squealed and cheered. Well, everyone except Dallas. She shot him a look that could stop most men dead in their tracks, but he wasn't most men.

Dallas stood from her stool and started toward them, and Bowie cursed. "Um, I'm pretty sure the shit is about to hit the fucking fan now, Savage," he said. Savage had a bad feeling that Bowie was right.

He held his breath, second-guessing every decision he had made that day, right down to asking Bowie out and buying Dallas' friends a round of drinks. Yep, he was thoroughly fucked and all he wanted to do was get the hell out of there. Savage stood and threw down a hundred-dollar bill, knowing that would cover his tab, and smiled at Bowie.

"That offer to get a beer at your place still stand?" Savage asked.

Bowie smiled and nodded. "Sure," he said. "But, for the record, you're being a chicken." He looked across the bar to where Dallas was making her way across the crowded dance floor and sighed. Bowie was right but he didn't give a fuck. Better to leave as a chicken than face his ex's wrath.

"Yep," he breathed. "Ready?" He held out his hand for Bowie, knowing he might be sending not only Dallas but everyone who was currently watching the exchange between them, a clear sign that the two of them were together.

Bowie took his hand, and they made their way to the front of the bar. Just as Savage stepped out of the doorway and into the night, he looked back to find Dallas watching him; frozen to her spot with her mouth gaping wide open. Yeah, she had gotten the message, loud and clear—he was leaving the bar with Bowie and there would be no backtracking now. There would be nothing he could do to erase the hatred and pain that he saw in her beautiful eyes.

DALLAS

Dallas St. James just about fell off her damn barstool when Savage walked into The Voodoo Lounge with the handsome guy in fatigues. The two made quite a pair and she wasn't the only female in the bar to notice them. Every woman in her group seemed to sit up and take notice of the new conquests as soon as they walked in, even the bride-to-be.

She thought she'd never see Savage again and that was just fine with her. They had dated for about a month and then nothing—he seemed to vanish off the face of the earth. It was her fault really. She never pushed to know more about him than his first name and the fact that he used to be in the Air Force. He had mentioned that he was a scientist, but Dallas worried that if she pushed for him to tell her more, he'd bolt. It was ironic, really. He ended up changing her life forever and then ghosting her, never to be heard from again—or so she thought.

Dallas was determined to steer clear of Savage and whoever the guy was that came into the bar with him, but then he went too far and bought the bridal party a round of drinks. Was he trying to get her attention? If he was, it worked. By the time she got her nerve up, Savage and the guy got up to leave but what she saw next—it couldn't have been right. The bar was crowded, and she had to have seen the whole thing wrong because if she wasn't mistaken, they were holding hands when they left the bar.

She tried to rejoin her girlfriends, but she just wasn't in the mood to party after seeing Savage. He dredged up everything she had worked so hard to suppress—her anger, her fears, and damn it, even her desires. How could she still want him like she did after the hell he'd put her through over the past year since he left her without a word? Sure, Savage didn't make her any pretty promises. She thought she meant more to him than just a fuck, but she was wrong. She had not only misjudged him but so many other things too.

Dallas bowed out of the rest of the night, not really in the mood for the strip club the girls were heading to next. All she could think about was getting back to her little apartment and shutting the world out until she could think straight again. Savage always seemed to have that effect on her—made her thoughts a little cloudy. Seeing him tonight just reminded her of the crazy, lust-filled month that they spent together, and she needed to put those thoughts and images out of her head. There would be no more remembering the man who controlled her body, mind, and soul. Savage threw her away and that was going to be the painful reminder she took home with her tonight. He didn't want her, and she'd do well to remember that.

Dallas climbed the two floors to her apartment and unlocked the door, letting herself in. "Hello," she whispered.

"Hey—did you have fun?" Her friend Eden poked her head around the corner and smiled. "I'm assuming that since you are home so early that my answer is no, but I thought I'd be polite and ask."

Dallas made a face and Eden softly cursed. "You saw him, didn't you? She asked. Her friend always was able to pick up things."

"How the hell did you figure that out?" Dallas grumbled.

"You make a face anytime his name is brought up. Listen, I've never met the guy, but you're going to have to get over this anger you're harboring towards him. If not for yourself then for Greer," Eden said.

Dallas sighed and nodded. Her friend was right—she owed it to both herself and her daughter to stop hating the man who had given her the greatest gift she ever had.

"I ran into him tonight at The Voodoo Lounge," Dallas admitted.

"Well, shit. That's not good. Did you talk to him?" Eden asked. Dallas could hear the question her friend was really asking her.

"Just go ahead and ask," Dallas said.

"Did you tell him about Greer?" Eden dramatically whispered.

Dallas shook her head. "No. I didn't even get the chance to talk to him. He was sitting across the bar with some really good-looking guy and by the time I tried to make it across the crowded dance floor, they bolted."

"Good," Eden said. "You don't owe him anything, Dallas. He used you and left you pregnant and alone. Hell, you didn't even know if that fucker was alive or dead. Telling him about Greer would be a huge mistake." Dallas wondered if her friend was right. For months after Savage cut off contact with her, she worried that he had been in some horrific accident and was hurt or worse—dead. It was silly really but believing some made up tragic story was so much easier than knowing the truth. He just walked away from her, and that realization stung like a son-of-a-bitch. Eden was right about one thing—Savage used her and didn't even have the common decency to tell her it was over. He was a coward, and he showed his true colors tonight when he ran out of that bar again.

"Maybe you're right," Dallas said with a shrug.

"No maybe about it, girl. You've proven that you don't need his damn help with Greer. You're an awesome mom and your daughter will get everything she needs from you and well—me, her fabulous auntie."

Dallas giggled, "Thanks, fabulous auntie," she teased. "I needed to hear that tonight. It was just so strange, you know?"

"You mean seeing him again?" Eden asked.

"No—the way he left out of that bar. First, he took off like his pants were on fire and then, I could have sworn that he was holding hands with the hot guy he was with."

"What?" Eden questioned. "As in—they were there together, on a date?"

"Yeah, but that's crazy, right?" Dallas asked. Maybe she hadn't seen them correctly or she had just misread the situation.

"Well, that would explain why he ghosted you," Eden offered. "Maybe he realized he liked being with guys," she teased.

"Are you implying that I turned him gay?" Dallas mocked upset and Eden giggled.

"That is one explanation," Eden joked, but Dallas found the whole topic less funny than her friend seemed to. Dallas had more at stake in all of this—she had more to lose and there would be no way she'd take chances with her daughter's happiness, not even for the sexiest man she had ever known. When Savage walked away from her, he didn't realize he was also leaving behind a little piece of himself that would remind Dallas, every day, of the time they had spent together. Her three-month-old daughter, Greer, was the spitting image of her father and the reason why she needed to work through her anger towards Savage. She owed her daughter at least that much.

Savage Heat (RBMC Book 1) Universal Link-> https://books2read.com/u/brq7pA

What's coming up next from K.L. Ramsey? Here's a sneak peek at Bekim (Garo Syndicate Trilogy Book 2)—coming on 4/19/22!

BEKIM

BEKIM GARO HAD ONE JOB TO DO. HE WAS GIVEN THE TASK OF moving one of the women sold at auction out of Albania and to the states where her new owner was waiting for her. His only problem was that every time the girl looked at him, he wanted to let her go and help her to escape the hell that she had been living for the past two months. He couldn't do that though, because if he did, he'd find himself in a shit ton of hot water—not only with his older brother, Edon but with the Tirana family who had hired him to deliver her.

He told Edon that he didn't want the job. Hell, he all but begged his older brother not to make him do it, but Edon insisted, saying that he owed the Tirana Syndicate a favor and this was his chance to pay them back and strike it off of their family's books. The one thing he knew about his older brother—he hated feeling that he owed anyone a debt. Edon paid back his promises and now, he was using Bekim to do it.

Bekim drove down to the Tirana warehouse to pick up the girl. He'd only seen her a handful of times when he'd go over there, delivering things for his brother. She had the bluest eyes he'd ever seen and when she looked at him, almost as if she was pleading with him for help, he found himself wanting to give it. He just had no idea that her life would literally be in his hands until he could deliver her to her new owner. He worried that he'd fuck it all up and give in to what his conscience was telling him to do every time that girl looked into his soul.

"She's a tricky girl," one of the Tirana goons said. "She acts all innocent, but she's full of venom. Be careful with that one," he said, nodding into her cage where she sat staring back at Bekim.

"I know how to do my fucking job," Bek spat. "You just worry about getting her papers in order so that I can get her to America. I'll handle the rest." The guy nodded, and walked away, mumbling something about Garo assholes in Albanian.

"Will you help me?" the woman whispered. He almost didn't turn around to look into her cage, knowing that those blue eyes would be staring back at him as if daring him to do the right fucking thing. He couldn't do as she requested—it would end up getting both of them killed.

Bekim sighed and turned to face her. "No," he whispered back. "You're a job, honey and I plan on doing my fucking job." He didn't miss the hint of disappointment in her eyes or the way that she defiantly smirked up at him as if she didn't believe a word he was saying.

"Right," she breathed, still staring him down. "Do you even want to know my name?" she asked. Knowing her name would give her more power over him. It would make her human and he couldn't let that happen. His brother told him not to get involved. Edon said to consider her goods and not a person—as if that would make any of this easier. Besides, he could see that she was a person and not merchandise that he was delivering to some asshole in America. What kind of sick, pervert bought women from another country and had them shipped, like cargo, to America? Bekim had a feeling that he didn't want to find out the answer to that question and neither would the woman sitting in the cage, staring back at him.

"No," he whispered. "Your name isn't important to me, and neither is your story. Just keep both to yourself. In fact, how about you just keep your mouth shut for the entire fucking trip, and we won't have any problems."

"You're just like them," she spat. "I should have known that your eyes were a lie."

"My eyes?" he asked. "What the hell does that mean?"

"You have kind eyes," she said. "At least, I thought you did. But you're just as much an asshole as the others. You know what—my name is Amra, and I won't be silent."

Bekim crossed the hallway to her cage and grabbed the bars, liking that she was smart enough to take a step back from him. He usually didn't give in to his rage, but this girl made him want to break all of his fucking rules.

"Well, princess," he said. "I'm betting that I can teach you to follow the rules, if necessary."

"My name isn't Amra, not princess," she corrected.

"Amra means princess," he insisted. "So, that's what I'm going to call you for our little trip." He turned to leave the cell room and didn't turn back when she called after him. Sure, she was calling him an asshole, but he hadn't shared his name as she so freely had. He wasn't about to give her any information about himself because letting her in would be a mistake—a huge mistake, and he wasn't going to let his family down.

AMRA

AMRA SPENT THE NIGHT WAITING FOR THE MAN TO COME BACK to collect her. She thought that they were going to move her right away, but she heard the guys talking about not having the correct forms to get her out of the country. That was fine with her since she didn't want to go to America anyway.

She still couldn't figure out what had happened over the past couple of months, which had landed her in a cell, waiting to be carted off to some rich, American asshole who had bought her. The last thing she remembered was being out to dinner with her older sister and her husband. They had a meal that just remembering it now, made her mouth water. She said goodbye to her sister and brother-in-law and used the restroom on her way out.

Everything seemed fine until she walked out into the

parking lot and found the trunk of her car open. She walked to the back of her car, to shut the trunk, and someone hit her on the head from behind and shoved her in, just before she lost consciousness. The very last thing she remembered was some guy with dark hair looking back in at her, and wanting to scream, but not being able to. And now, she was being held in a cage, sold off as a sex slave to an American businessman, and worried that she'd never see her sister again.

"Hey," she shouted, trying to get the guard's attention. "I'm thirsty." It had been so long since she had actual food—almost two days, and they weren't very good about giving her water either. Honestly, they were giving her just enough food and water to keep her alive before having to transport her. Maybe they did it to keep her week, but she still felt as though she had a lot of fight left in her.

"Hey," she shouted again. The blond guard looked back over his shoulder at her, his smile mean.

"You want something to drink?" he taunted.

"Yes, please," she begged. "Can I please have some water?"

He tossed a bottle of water into her cage, and she picked it up off of the floor. "You ask me nice like that and I'll give you anything you want," he offered, leaning on the bars to her cage. She knew exactly what he was offering her, but she would rather die than take him up on his offer.

"All right," she said. "How about letting me go back to my life then?" she asked.

"Can't do that, honey," he said. "Your new master is

waiting to meet you and as soon as Garo gets his ass back in here, we'll be able to send you on your way." He said that to her as if he expected her to be excited about what was about to happen to her. She was the opposite of excited. Amra was terrified, but she wouldn't tell him that.

"This is good for you," the guard insisted.

"Oh?" she asked. "How so?"

"You were a second-grade teacher, right?" he asked.

She didn't answer his question. She hadn't told them anything about her personal life, believing that the less they knew about her, the better. But they still seemed to know things that they shouldn't about her. He could tell that she was avoiding answering his question, laughing at her trying to ignore him.

"It's all right," he said. "I already know all about you, honey," he said.

"I don't give a fuck what you think you know about me, asshole," she spat, causing him to laugh at her again.

"You keep some of that spunk, honey. You're going to need it for your long trip to America," he said. "Plus, I'm sure that your new owner will want to have some fun with you and try out his goods once you get there. You're going to need all the energy that you can muster," he taunted. "I wish that I was the one taking you to America, I'd get you good and ready for your new owner before handing you over, honey." The thought of him touching her made her physically ill.

Amra had never been touched by any man, for that matter, and the thought of her first time being forced pissed her off. She was saving herself for the right guy, which was laughable now. There was no such thing as the right man for her and it was time for her to stop living in a fantasy world. She had to find a way out of her cage before this Garo guy came back to pick her up.

When she didn't acknowledge the guard's disgusting remark, he seemed to get bored and left her. She liked it better when they would just leave her alone, but then, she was left with her thoughts and that wasn't much better. She sat down on her cot and drank down the water more quickly than she should have.

"You ready to get on the road?" the same man from earlier asked from the corner of the room, holding up what she assumed were the papers that they were working on to get her out of the country.

"No," she breathed. "But I'm assuming that you're not asking me, really."

"Correct," he agreed. He nodded to one of the guards and she was released from her cage. She felt herself clutching the empty bottle of water as if it was her lifeline.

"I won't go quietly," she said.

"So you told me earlier," the guy reminded. "I don't care if you scream your head off for the entire flight. I have noise-canceling earbuds and own a private jet. Scream yourself hoarse," he offered. Of course, they weren't going to transport her all the way to America on a commercial flight. They would be found out for being human traffickers, and she had a feeling that they were smart about not being caught.

"Well, Garo," she said. "I plan on making your life as miserable as possible while I have to be in your company."

He chuckled and looked her over. "They said you were spunky. I'm betting that one of the guards told you my last name then?" he asked. She looked over to the guard who had spilled the beans and loved the way that the guy seemed to turn a little green from being called out.

"No matter," he said. "You can call me Mr. Garo then." There was no way that she'd dignify calling him mister anything, but she wasn't about to tell him that. From the way that the guards seemed to cower in his presence, he wasn't a man who many choose to fuck with. Good thing she never really gave a shit about what other people did or didn't do.

"Shall we?" she asked, holding up her bound wrists to him, still clutching the empty water bottle. "Garo," she quickly added. He barked out his laugh and smiled down at her. He was quite a bit bigger than she was and easily towered over her.

"This is going to be fun," he whispered into her ear, causing her to shiver. She hated that he had that effect on her, but the fact that she found her dark, mysterious captor handsome wasn't her problem or her fault. What Amra needed to remember was that she had hours, not days, to find her way free from Mr. Garo. Otherwise, she was going to end up living the life of a captive sex slave and that wasn't her plan—not by a long shot.

Bekim (Garo Syndicate Trilogy Book 2) Universal Link->
https://books2read.com/u/m0lepY

ABOUT K.L. RAMSEY & BE KELLY

Romance Rebel fighting for
Happily Ever After!

K. L. Ramsey currently resides in West Virginia (Go Mountaineers!). In her spare time, she likes to read romance novels, go to WVU football games and attend book club (aka-drink wine) with girlfriends. K. L. enjoys writing Contemporary Romance, Erotic Romance, and Sexy Ménage! She loves to write strong, capable women and bossy, hot as hell alphas, who fall ass over tea kettle for them. And of course, her stories always have a happy ending. But wait—there's more!

Somewhere along the writing path, K.L. developed a love of ALL things paranormal (but has a special affinity for shifters <YUM!!>)!! She decided to take a chance and create another persona- BE Kelly- to bring you all of her yummy shifters, seers, and everything paranormal (plus a hefty dash of MC!).

K. L. RAMSEY'S SOCIAL MEDIA

Ramsey's Rebels - K.L. Ramsey's Readers Group
https://www.facebook.com/groups/ramseysrebels

KL Ramsey & BE Kelly's ARC Team
https://www.facebook.com/groups/klramseyandbekellyarcteam

KL Ramsey and BE Kelly's Newsletter
https://mailchi.mp/4e73ed1b04b9/authorklramsey/

KL Ramsey and BE Kelly's Website
https://www.klramsey.com

- facebook.com/kl.ramsey.58
- instagram.com/itsprivate2
- bookbub.com/profile/k-l-ramsey
- twitter.com/KLRamsey5
- amazon.com/K.L.-Ramsey/e/B0799P6JGJ

BE KELLY'S SOCIAL MEDIA

BE Kelly's Reader's group
https://www.facebook.com/
groups/kellsangelsreadersgroup/

- facebook.com/be.kelly.564
- instagram.com/bekellyparanormalromanceauthor
- twitter.com/BEKelly9
- bookbub.com/profile/be-kelly
- amazon.com/BE-Kelly/e/B081LLD38M

WORKS BY K. L. RAMSEY

The Relinquished Series Box Set

Love Times Infinity

Love's Patient Journey

Love's Design

Love's Promise

Harvest Ridge Series Box Set

Worth the Wait

The Christmas Wedding

Line of Fire

Torn Devotion

Fighting for Justice

Last First Kiss Series Box Set

Theirs to Keep

Theirs to Love

Theirs to Have

Theirs to Take

Second Chance Summer Series

True North

The Wrong Mister Right

Ties That Bind Series

Saving Valentine

Blurred Lines

Dirty Little Secrets

Ties That Bind Box Set

Taken Series

Double Bossed

Double Crossed

Double The Mistletoe

Double Down

Owned

His Secret Submissive

His Reluctant Submissive

His Cougar Submissive

His Nerdy Submissive

His Stubborn Submissive- Coming soon!

Alphas in Uniform

Hellfire

Royal Bastards MC

Savage Heat

Whiskey Tango

Can't Fix Cupid

Ratchet's Revenge

Patched for Christmas

Love at First Fight

Dizzy's Desire

Savage Hell MC Series

Roadkill

REPOssession

Dirty Ryder

Hart's Desire

Axel's Grind

Razor's Edge

Lone Star Rangers

Don't Mess With Texas

Sweet Adeline

Dash of Regret

Austin's Starlet

Ranger's Revenge

Smokey Bandits MC Series

Aces Wild

Queen of Hearts

Full House

King of Clubs

Joker's Wild

Tirana Brothers (Social Rejects Syndicate

Llir

Altin

Veton

Dirty Desire Series

Torrid

Clean Sweep

Mountain Men Mercenary Series

Eagle Eye

Hacker

Widowmaker

Deadly Sins Syndicate (Mafia Series)

Pride

Envy

Greed

Lust

Wrath- Coming soon!

Sloth- Coming soon!

Gluttony- Coming soon!

Forgiven Series

Confession of a Sinner

Confessions of a Saint

Confessions of a Rebel- Coming soon!

Chasing Serendipity Series

Kismet

Sealed With a Kiss Series

Kissable

Garo Syndicate Trilogy

Edon

Bekim

Rovena- Coming soon!

Billionaire Boys Club

His Naughty Assistant

His Virgin Assistant

His Nerdy Assistant

His Curvy Assistant

His Bossy Assistant

His Rebellious Assistant

Grumpy Mountain Men Series

Grizz

The Bridezilla Series

Happily Ever After- Almost

Rope 'Em and Ride 'Em Series

Saddle Up- Coming soon!

Craving the Cowboy- Coming soon!

WORKS BY BE KELLY (K.L.'S ALTER EGO...)

Reckoning MC Seer Series

Reaper

Tank

Raven

Reckoning MC Series Box Set

Perdition MC Shifter Series

Ringer

Rios

Trace

Perdition 3 Book Box Set

Wren's Pack- Coming soon!

Silver Wolf Shifter Series

Daddy Wolf's Little Seer

Daddy Wolf's Little Captive

Daddy Wolf's Little Star

Rogue Enforcers

Juno

Blaze- Coming soon

Elite Enforcers

A Very Rogue Christmas Novella

One Rogue Turn

Graystone Academy Series

Eden's Playground

Violet's Surrender- Coming soon!

Holly's Hope (A Christmas Novella)- Coming soon!

Renegades Shifter Series

Pandora's Promise

Kinsley's Pact

Leader of the Pack Series

Wren's Pack

Printed in Great Britain
by Amazon